THE
KINGFISHER TREASURY OF
Princess Stories

CHOSEN BY FIONA WATERS

ILLUSTRATED BY PATRICE AGGS

KINGFISHER

NEW YOR

D0499511

CONTENTS

KINGFISHER TREASURIES

A *wealth of stories to share!*

Ideal for reading aloud with younger children, or for more experienced readers to enjoy independently, **Kingfisher Treasuries** offer a wonderful range of the very best writing for children. Carefully selected by an expert compiler, each collection reflects the real interests and enthusiasms of children. Stories by favorite classic and contemporary authors appear alongside traditional folk tales and fables in a lively mix of writing drawn from many cultures around the world.

Generously illustrated throughout, **Kingfisher Treasuries** guarantee hours of the highest quality entertainment and, by introducing them to new authors, encourage children to further develop their reading tastes.

For Bryher—a proper Princess
with much love—F. W.

For Ismay Rymaszewska—P. A.

KINGFISHER
a Houghton Mifflin Company imprint
215 Park Avenue South
New York, New York 10003
www.houghtonmifflinbooks.com

First published in 2001
2 4 6 8 10 9 7 5 3
2TR/0102/THOM/(MA)/INDWF115

LIBRARY OF CONGRESS CATALOGING–IN–PUBLICATION DATA
has been applied for.

0-7534-5374-6

Printed in India

THE PRINCESS AND THE FROG

Brothers Grimm
Retold by Vivian French

The King and the Queen were going out to tea. They looked anxiously at Princess Crystal.

"You will be good, won't you, precious?" said the King.

"Yes, Father," said Crystal.

"And you won't order all the guards to run egg-and-spoon races?" said the Queen.

"No, Mother," said Crystal.

"Or paint spots on the royal horses?" said the King.

Crystal sighed. "No, Father."

"And you won't play near the well, will you, Crystal?" said the Queen.

Crystal yawned. "No, Mother," she said.

"And you'll do just what the Prime Minister tells you to do?" said the King.

Crystal rolled her big blue eyes. "Father," she said, "I promise I'll be as good as gold—sure as eggs is eggs." And she sat herself down on the golden throne with a flump.

"Well," said the King. "I suppose it'll be all right." He turned to the Prime Minister, who was hovering in a corner. "You won't let her out of your sight for even a second, will you, PM?"

"Indeed not, Your Majesty," said the Prime Minister.

"Heigh-ho," said the King. "I suppose we'd better be off, then."

"I suppose we had," said the Queen. "Good-bye, my darling girl."

"Cheerio," said Crystal. "Oh! Can I play with that while you're gone?" She pointed to a large golden ball on a table near the throne.

"No, my dear," said the King. "That is my royal orb."

"Your royal what?" Crystal asked.

"Orb," said the King. "It goes with my scepter."

He puffed out his chest. "They are what make me a king. Those and my crown."

"Oh." Crystal frowned. "It doesn't look very special. It's only a golden ball. Can't I play with it just for a little while? I could play lawn bowling."

The King and the Queen looked horrified. "No no no!" they said together.

"Promise you won't touch it, Crystal dear," said the King, "and we'll bring you an extra specially lovely present."

"Okay," said Crystal. "I promise—sure as eggs is eggs."

"There's my darling girlie pearlie," said the Queen. "Come along, King. We mustn't be late!"

When the King and the Queen had gone, Crystal jumped up.

"Have they really gone, PM?" she asked.

The Prime Minister peered out of the window, and nodded.

"Good," said Crystal. "Usual plan?"

The Prime Minister nodded again. "If that is your wish, Princess."

"It is," said Crystal. "I'll go and play in the garden, and you can go and have tea with Cook."

The Prime Minister's head almost touched the shiny marble floor, he bowed so low. "Thank you, Princess. An excellent arrangement, if I may say so."

Crystal waited until the Prime Minister had walked down the corridor and into the royal kitchen. As soon as the kitchen door had swung shut she picked up the golden orb, stuffed it into her pocket, and skipped out into the palace garden.

Once she was in the garden Crystal headed straight for the well. There were so many interesting things to see there, and it was fun dropping stones into the deep black depths and hearing them *kersplosh!* at the bottom. Also the well was out of sight of the kitchen window, so she could play with the golden ball without being seen. . . .

Crystal began by rolling the ball, but it didn't roll straight. She tried bouncing it, but it was too solid to bounce. She tried throwing it up in the air and catching it, but it was too heavy to go high.

"Bother," said Crystal, and she tossed the ball away.

SPLASH!

"Oh," said Crystal. "Oh, no. Oh, bother. Oh, goodness me. Oh . . . HELP!"

She leaned over the top of the well and peered down . . . but there was no sign of the ball. Only a circle of ripples showed where it had fallen.

"I think," Crystal said to herself, "I'm in trouble. BAD trouble. In fact, I think I'm in the worst trouble I've ever ever been in. Oh, bother!" And she swallowed hard to stop herself from bursting into tears.

"Ahem."

Crystal spun around.

"Ahem."

A small speckled frog was sitting close beside her.

"Excuse me," said the frog, "but I couldn't help noticing that you look rather upset."

Crystal nodded. She couldn't quite speak yet.

"Am I right in thinking that you dropped something?" The frog gave her a sideways look. "I did hear a splash."

Crystal nodded again. "It was a golden ball," she said, and her voice wobbled. "It's my father's orb. He says it's one of the things that makes him a king."

"Oh dear." The frog shook his head. "I can understand you feel a little anxious. Would you like me to fetch it for you?"

Crystal stared at him. "What?"

The frog looked a little taken aback. "I am a frog, you know. I can swim."

"Oh, yes." Crystal rubbed her eyes. "Could you—could you really fetch it for me?"

"Of course." The frog hopped a little nearer. "Naturally there'll be the usual payment?"

"Payment?" said Crystal.

"A kiss," the frog said. "I fetch your father's very special golden orb—and you give me a kiss."

Crystal smiled her best blue-eyed princess smile. "I promise that I'll give you a kiss—sure as eggs is eggs."

"Excellent," said the frog, and he dived into the well.

He was back in no time at all. "Here you are," he said, pushing the ball toward her. "It's a little wet—but as good as new."

"Thank you!" said Crystal, and she leaned down and took the ball. "Thank you—and good-bye!" And she gave the frog a push.

SPLASH!

"Nasty slimy thing!" said Crystal and, clutching the golden ball, she ran as fast as she could all the way back to the palace.

When the King and the Queen came home they found her playing tic-tac-toe with the Prime Minister and the Cook.

The doorbell rang just as Crystal was finishing her supper. The Prime Minister went to see who it was and came back looking most surprised.

"Excuse me, Princess," he said. "It's for you."

The King looked up from his plate of bread and cheese. "Who is it? It's very late!"

The Prime Minister shifted from foot to foot. "Ah . . . it's a frog," he said.

"A frog?" said the King. "What does a frog want with the Princess?"

"Nasty slimy thing," said the Queen. "Send it away!"

"Yes," said Crystal. "Send it away!"

The Prime Minister bowed, and walked away to the front door.

"Really," said the King. "What audacity!"

Half an hour later the doorbell rang again, this time much louder.

"Dear me," said the Queen. "Whoever can that be?"

"Some people have no consideration," said the King.

Crystal said nothing. She had an odd feeling in her stomach.

Again the Prime Minister went to see who it was. He came back frowning.

"It's the frog again, Your Majesties," he said. "He says the Princess has something that belongs to him."

"No I haven't," Crystal said quickly. "Tell him to go away."

The Prime Minister bowed, and went off to the front door.

The King was reading Crystal a bedtime story when the knocking began. It was so loud that Crystal jumped, and the King dropped the book.

"Should we call the guard?" asked the Queen nervously.

"Perhaps we should, Your Majesty," said the Prime Minster.

"Yes!" Crystal said. "Yes! Call the guard!"

"No no no! I'll go and see who it is," said the King.

Crystal felt the feeling in her stomach get worse. She was almost sure she knew who it was . . . and when the King went marching toward the front door she tiptoed behind him.

Sure enough the frog was sitting on the doorstep.

"Now then," the King began. "Enough is enough! If you don't hop along this minute—"

"Excuse me," the frog interrupted, "I don't mean to be a nuisance, but I did a little favor for the Princess. She was playing by the—"

"WAIT!" Crystal jumped in front of the King. "It's all right, Father. We were . . . we were playing a little game. It's my fault. I promised him a kiss, but I didn't ever do it . . . but I will now. Come here, you nasty slimy thing."

And Crystal took a deep breath, bent down, and kissed the frog.

BOINGGGGGGGG!

There was a strange humming noise . . . and the frog grew . . . and grew . . . and GREW . . . into the handsomest prince Crystal had ever seen.

"WOW!" said Crystal.

"Goodness me!" said the King.

"Won't you come in?" said the Queen.

The Prince sank to one knee and held out his arms to Crystal.

"Dear Princess," he said, "you have broken the spell."

Crystal was speechless.

"I promise," said the Prince, "that one day, when you are older, I will come riding up on a snow-white horse to carry you away to my royal kingdom."

Crystal looked thoughtful as she dropped him a curtsy. "Thanks," she said. "And I promise that I'll be here waiting for you—just as sure as eggs is eggs."

THE PRINCESS'S HANDKERCHIEFS

Margaret Baker

The Princess Darling had everything she wanted. She had gardens full of beautiful flowers, and rooms full of beautiful clothes, and cupboards and cupboards full of the most wonderful books and toys to be found in all the world. She ought to have been happy from morning to night, but it was so exceedingly dull to have everything given to her before she had time to wish for it that she used to burst into tears a dozen times a day, and the King had to build a special laundry and hire a new laundrymaid for no other purpose than to wash the Princess's handkerchiefs.

"Do stop crying, Darling!" the Queen would beg. "If only you'll tell us what you want you shall have it at once!"

"But that's the worst of it!" whimpered Darling. "I don't *know* what I want! If I knew I'd stop!"

At last the Princess grew so used to crying that she cried all the time. She began in the morning the moment she wakened, and she cried till she fell asleep again at night. She had a lady-in-waiting who had nothing to do but help her dry her tears, and four little pages who ran backward and forward between the palace and the laundry all day long, taking bundles of dripping handkerchiefs to be washed and bringing back neat piles of clean ones.

The poor little laundrymaid had not a moment to herself; however busily she washed and rinsed and dried and ironed, there were always bundles and bundles of tear-soaked handkerchiefs waiting to be done.

"It's just too silly for anything!" she sniffed. "Fancy crying like that because you don't know what you want! I know what the Princess wants— she wants a good shaking! And I know what *I* want, too; I want a holiday. It's too bad I should have to work here day after day with never a chance of enjoying myself—I might as well be shut up in the palace dungeons!"

So the Princess wept into gold-embroidered pocket-handkerchiefs, and the laundrymaid wept into the washtubs, and it was very damp and uncomfortable for everybody.

One fine windy morning the little laundress wakened with the first streak of dawn and jumped out of bed, for there were such numbers of wet handkerchiefs waiting to be washed that she had not a moment to lose. The wind blew her hair from under her cap and flapped her apron about her ankles as she ran to the laundry, but she did not mind in the least. "It will be a grand morning for drying!" she thought.

She filled the tubs with water and washed and rinsed with such haste that the largest clothes basket was soon piled with handkerchiefs all ready to be pegged out to dry; in fact it was piled so high that she could hardly see over it when she picked it up, and before she had carried it half a dozen steps beyond the laundry door she tripped over a stone. Down fell the basket and down fell the laundrymaid, and in less than no time the handkerchiefs were flying away on the wind.

"Oh! Oh! Oh!" shrieked the little laundrymaid, picking herself up, and she began to run after them.

The handkerchiefs blew over the fence into the meadow where a cowherd was minding the royal cattle. The cows stuck their tails into the air and ran away, and the cowherd stood staring with his mouth wide open.

"That's a queer flock of birds!" said he.

"It isn't a flock of birds!" cried the little laundrymaid. "It's the Princess's handkerchiefs blowing away!"

"Why, who'd have thought it!" exclaimed the cowherd, and he helped the laundrymaid across the fence and they ran across the meadow together.

The handkerchiefs fluttered far ahead and blew over the brook onto the common, where the parson was walking up and down thinking over next Sunday's sermon.

"Dear me! What curious clouds!" he exclaimed.

"They're not clouds!" cried the little laundrymaid.

"They're the Princess's handkerchiefs blowing away!"

"Dear ME!" cried the parson. "How extraordinary!" And he pulled his hat firmly over his ears and began to run too.

The handkerchiefs flapped all the way across the common and over the stile into the road just as the children were going past on their way to school.

"Butterflies! Oh, what big ones!" they shouted.

"They're the Princess's handkerchiefs! Catch them, catch them!" shrieked the laundrymaid.

"Hurrah!" shouted the children, for a handkerchief chase was much more fun than going to school, and they ran after the laundrymaid and the cowherd and the parson.

The wind had never had such a capital frolic before. It danced the handkerchiefs along the village street and into the blacksmith's yard, and out of the yard into the miller's orchard, and across the orchard into a turnip field, and over the hedge into the road again, and through the great marble arch into the palace gardens themselves. No sooner did anyone see the fluttering, dancing cloud than they stopped to stare; and no sooner did they hear the little laundress pant, "It's the—Princess's—handker—chiefs!" than they began to run after her—the lawyer and the doctor, the baker and the pieman, the seamstress and the henwife, the pedlar and the beggar, the goose-girl, and the chimney sweep, and so many more that they could not be counted.

And all this while the Princess Darling sat in her room and cried and cried and cried.

"Run to the royal laundry and bring me some clean handkerchiefs," whispered the lady-in-waiting to the first little page.

The page stuck his velvet cap on the back of his head and hurried away, but when he reached the laundry there was nobody there. He looked inside, but all he could see were tubs of water and bundles of wet handkerchiefs; he looked outside, and there he saw the laundrymaid running across the fields and chasing a little white cloud.

"Bless my gold braid and buttons!" exclaimed the page. "I do believe the clean handkerchiefs have all blown away!" And he set off to join in the chase as fast as his legs could carry him.

And still the Princess cried and cried.

When the first page did not return, the lady-in-waiting beckoned the second one to her side.

"Run to the royal laundry—do not waste a minute—and bring the clean handkerchiefs!" she ordered.

The page ran to the laundry just as he was bidden, but there were no clean handkerchiefs ready for him. He stood in the doorway shading his eyes with his hand as he looked for the laundrymaid, and it was not long before he saw her, far away down the road, chasing a little white cloud with a crowd of people running at her heels.

"Bless my wig!" he exclaimed. "The handkerchiefs are blowing away!" And *he* ran after the laundrymaid too.

The lady-in-waiting sent

the third page after the second, and the fourth after the third, and when none of them returned and there was only one clean handkerchief left she picked up her embroidered satin skirts and set out to run to the royal laundry herself.

The Princess was so miserable she did not notice that anything had gone wrong. She took the last clean handkerchief and held it to her eyes, and her tears were so big that it instantly became as wet as if she had dropped it in the goldfish pool. She tossed it on one side and stretched out her hand for another, but there was no handkerchief there. Such a thing had never happened before, and it was so astonishing that the Princess opened her eyes and looked around. There was no lady-in-waiting, there were no pages, and the only handkerchiefs to be seen were the very, very wet ones strewn around her on the floor.

She opened the door and ran out into the corridor. "I want some clean handkerchiefs!" she called; but nobody heard her, for by this time the wind was blowing the handkerchiefs around and around the palace gardens and everybody but the King and Queen and the Princess herself had hurried out to join in the chase.

"I want some clean handkerchiefs!" she called again, running along the corridor, but still nobody answered. She ran through the great hall, and onto the terrace that overlooked the palace gardens.

"I want some clean handkerchiefs!" she called once
more.

Just as though they had heard her a cloud of
handkerchiefs came dancing overhead and fluttered
to the ground like enormous snowflakes. Before
she could say anything in her surprise the little
laundrymaid came panting around the corner, and
after the laundrymaid came the cowherd, and after
the cowherd came the parson, and after the parson
came the school children and the lawyer and
the doctor and the baker and the pieman and the
seamstress and the henwife and the pedlar and

the beggar and the goose-girl and the chimney sweep and the pages and the lady-in-waiting and all the palace servants from the turnspit to the Lord Controller of the Household in his powdered wig and gold and silver cloak. No sooner did they see the handkerchiefs on the ground than they all began to trip and stumble over each other in their eagerness to pick them up, and no sooner had they picked them up than they caught sight of the Princess on the terrace and they all began to trip and stumble over each other afresh in their eagerness to offer the handkerchiefs to her. Such a collection of crumpled, muddy, tattered handkerchiefs had surely never been seen before!

"But I want a clean one!" said the Princess, and suddenly found herself beginning to laugh.

The King and Queen came hurrying out to see what all the noise could mean. It was very surprising to see the royal gardens crowded with people who were all very breathless and red in the face, but it was much more surprising to see the Princess laughing as merrily as though she did it every day.

"What's this?" exclaimed the King. "Do you know what you want at last?"

"I want a clean handkerchief," said Darling.

"I had to stop crying because I couldn't possibly manage without a handkerchief to wipe away the tears—it would be too horrid to feel them trickling down my cheeks and off the end of my chin!"

The little laundrymaid pushed her way to the front. "I'll wash some straight away, Your Majesties," she said in a very frightened voice and curtsying very fast, for she was sure she was going to get into trouble for her carelessness. "The Princess shall have some clean handkerchiefs in half an hour!"

"Do you think I want her to start crying again?" exclaimed the King. "The Princess's handkerchiefs must remain unwashed forever and ever!"

"Then shall I be able to have a holiday?" cried the little laundrymaid.

"Everybody shall have a holiday," said the King, "and we'll all live happily ever after!"

And that is exactly what they did.

MOUSEY AND SULKY PUSS

Geraldine McCaughrean

"Hear ye! Hear ye! Let it be known in every corner of the land that a daughter is born to the King and Queen of Bellepays! Let no one work today, for the King declares this a public holiday!"

At the sound of the herald's announcement, everyone ran out into the streets and began to dance and sing. But when the invitations were sent out for the royal christening of the baby Princess, a terrible mistake was made.

No one invited Agatha!

Agatha had not always been a crabbed and spiteful witch. But ever since the day she turned her sister by mistake into a large black cat, Agatha had not smiled. Neither had her sister, come to that. In fact her sister was such a sad sack of a cat that she was known as Sulky Puss. Agatha searched

29

the world over for a magic spell that would restore her sister to human form, and it was while she was away on one such trip that Princess Marcia was born. That's why *no one invited Agatha.*

On the day of the christening, all manner of important and famous people traveled to the celebrations. So did Agatha. She waited until all the other christening presents had been given—spoons and egg cups and china bowls—then she did her worst.

"Because you made little of me, I shall make little of your precious Princess!" cried Agatha, and struck the crib with her wand. When the purple smoke cleared, Agatha had gone, and there in the cradle wriggled—a small white mouse.

The Mouse Princess they called her—or Mousey for short. And Mousey was very, very short. Her dresses could be made from a single silk handkerchief, her bed from an open jewel box.

 She was as pleasant a little thing as you could ever hope to meet —but she was, when all's said, a white mouse who ate cheese with her paws and whiffled her small, pink nose.

The King, terrified for her safety, banished every single cat from Bellepays, with one single exception. Sulky Puss, the witch's sister, was allowed to stay because no one dared tell her to go. Besides, she was a vegetarian.

As the years passed, the other baby girls in Bellepays grew into lovely young women. But Mousey only grew into a lovely young mouse. When she was in a room, it was easy to overlook her, to forget she was there. She squeaked so quietly that she was rarely heard. And not everyone was as kind and as loving as the King and Queen. Some were ashamed to admit they had a mouse for a Princess, and did their best to forget all about her. Just as Agatha had not been invited to the christening, *no one invited Mousey anywhere.*

Then, as in all such stories and histories, the Prince of the next-door kingdom announced his wish to choose a bride.

"Oyez! Oyez! Every maiden of wealth or degree is invited to the palace of the King of Oystria, so that the Prince Michelangelo may have dancing partners at the Grand Ball!"

What lines there were at the dress shops, at the milliners, the hairdressers, and the florists! There were carriages at every door and women arrayed in every color of the rainbow scrambling to be ready in time for the Grand Ball.

"I should like to go, too," said Mousey, but nobody heard her. She climbed onto the dinner table and shouted as loud as she was able, "I want to go, too!"

"Nonsense, Mousey, dear," said the Queen. "You would get trodden on."

"Besides, there are still cats in Oystria," said the King. "Out of the question. Get down off the table, please."

But the more they said no, the more determined Mousey became to go to the Ball. She put on her finest silk handkerchief dress—it was scarlet with silver embroidery—and a sash made from a velvet hair ribbon. She fetched a pin—to use as a sword if she met any cats—and put on her tiny tiara, then ran to the palace door.

But she was only in time to see the coach, with her mother and father in it, gathering speed as it drove away from the palace down the long, dusty drive.

Mousey sat down and wept.

Then she got up and dried her tears. How could she make the journey to Oystria? By boat?

She found her father's newspaper and folded it ever so many times, until she had made a paper boat. She dragged it to the moat and rowed it out to where the moat joined the winding river, which flowed right across both countries. But she had forgotten—the river flowed OUT of Oystria and INTO Bellepays. It was running in the wrong direction!

Mousey paddled ashore and thought again. She would fly to Oystria! But though she was able to fold a paper glider out of the newspaper, she could not get it up the winding stairs to the castle parapet.

She went to the stable, where the royal horses were kept. But the huge mares and stallions towered over her like monsters, and she dared not stay among those swinging hooves for fear she may be trampled and never seen again.

"What I need is a horse more suited to my size," thought Mousey, and as she crept out of the stable door, she saw the very thing.

A dozen chickens were pecking in the yard, and there beside the dung heap, a splendid red cockerel stretched its claws and surveyed its farmyard kingdom.

Mousey took the sash from her dress, ran full tilt up the dung heap, and launched herself onto the back of the cockerel. The bird was so startled that it set off to run. And after Mousey had got the ribbon into its beak for reins, it was just a matter of guiding the speeding fowl in the direction of the Oystrian border.

The Grand Ball was well underway when Mousey arrived, riding her cockerel. She did not dismount at the gate, nor at the steps, for fear the footmen and flunkies thought she was an ordinary house mouse. Indoors, she came to a scarlet-carpeted staircase lit by chandeliers. At the foot of the stairs, she could just make out the Prince.

She missed seeing Sulky Puss.

Oh yes, Sulky Puss was there. The King of Oystria had not made the same mistake as his neighbor. He had remembered to invite Agatha, and Agatha had brought her cat.

Sulky Puss saw the cockerel with its reins of scarlet velvet. She saw the meal-sized white mouse on its back, damp at the hems, stained black with newsprint, tiara awry over her little pink eyes, pin-sized sword raised aloft, and tiny mouth open to shout: "Out of the way! Out of the way! I don't know how to stop this bird!"

It was enough to make a cat laugh.

And that's just what Sulky Puss did. For the first time in her miserable sad-sack cat's nine lives, Sulky Puss rolled on her back in fits of giggles.

The music in the ballroom faltered and fell silent.

Everyone stared. For there, rolling on her back on the staircase, in a most unladylike way, was a large fat witch, laughing and laughing and laughing.

"Sister!" cried Agatha joyously. "The spell! It's lifted!"

"All I needed was a good laugh," said Anastasia, wiping her eyes and scratching some cat food off her dress. "And that sight was enough to give me one!"

Agatha looked down to see what jester or clown had restored her sister to her. And when she recognized the Mouse Princess, she was filled with tender remorse for the unkindness she had done at the christening.

And she hit Mousey with her wand.

The white mouse flew through the air, somersaulting one, two, three times before landing at the feet of the Prince of Oystria. She landed heavily, perhaps because she was no longer a mouse but a tall, elegant, pale-skinned girl in a ball dress of red silk, with ash-blonde hair tumbling down from a buckled tiara.

"Good gracious," said the Prince. "You are the most beautiful young lady I have seen all night. Will you marry me?"

"No, thank you," said Marcia, "I just wanted to dance."

So that's what they did instead.

THE WRESTLING PRINCESS

Judy Corbalis

Once upon a time there was a princess who was six feet tall, who liked her own way, and who loved to wrestle. Every day she would challenge the guards at her father's palace to wrestling matches and every day she won. Then she would pick up the loser and fling him on the ground, but gently, because she had a very kind nature.

The princess had one other unusual hobby. She liked to drive forklift trucks. Because she was a princess, and her father was very rich, she had three forklift trucks of her own—a blue one, a yellow one, and a green and purple striped one with a coronet on each side. Whenever there was a royal parade, the king would ride in front in his golden carriage, behind him would ride a company of soldiers, and behind them came the princess driving her striped royal forklift truck.

The king got very cross about it but the princess simply said, "If I can't drive my forklift truck, I won't go," and because she was such a good wrestler, the king was too scared to disagree with her.

One day, when the princess had wrestled with sixteen soldiers at once and had beaten them all, the king sent a page to tell her to come and see him in the royal tearoom.

The princess was annoyed.

"Is it urgent?" she asked the page. "I was just greasing the axle of my blue forklift truck."

"I think you should come, Your Highness," said the page, respectfully. "His Majesty was in a terrible temper. He's burnt four pieces of toast already and dripped butter all over his second-best ermine robe."

"Oh, gosh," said the princess, "I'd better come right away."

So she got up, picked up her oil can and went into the royal bathroom to wash her hands for tea. She left oil marks all over the gold taps and the page sent a message to the palace housekeeper to clean them quickly before the king saw them.

The princess went down to the tearoom and knocked loudly on the door. A herald opened it. "The Princess Ermyntrude!" he announced.

"About time, too," said the king. "And where have you been?"

"Greasing the axle of the blue forklift truck," answered the princess politely.

The king put his head in his hands and groaned.

"This can't go on," he sighed tragically. "When *will* you stop messing about with these dirty machines, Ermyntrude? You're nearly sixteen and you need a husband. I must have a successor."

"I'll succeed you, Father," cried the princess cheerfully. "I'd love to be a king."

"You can't be a king," said the king sadly. "It's not allowed."

"Why not?" asked the princess.

"I don't know," said the king. "I don't make the laws. Ask the judges—it's their affair. Anyway, you can't and that's that. You have to have a husband."

He picked up his tapestry and moodily started sewing.

"Ermyntrude," he said after a long silence, "you won't get a husband if you don't change your ways."

"Why ever not?" asked the princess, in surprise.

"To get a husband you must be enchantingly beautiful, dainty, and weak," said the king.

"Well, I'm not," said Ermyntrude cheerfully. "I'm nothing to look at, I'm six feet tall, and I'm certainly not weak. Why, Father, did you hear, this morning I wrestled with sixteen guards at once and I defeated them all?"

"Ermyntrude!" said the king sternly, as he rethreaded his needle with No. 9 blue tapestry cotton. "Ermyntrude, we are not having any more wrestling and no more forklift trucks either. If you want a husband, you will have to become delicate and frail."

"I *don't* want a husband," said the princess and she stamped her foot hard. The toast-rack wobbled. "*You* want me to have a husband. I just want to go on wrestling and looking after my trucks and driving in parades."

"Well, you can't," said the king. "And that's that. I shall lock up the forklift trucks and instruct the guards that there is to be no more wrestling and we shall have a contest to find you a husband."

The princess was furiously angry.

"Just you wait," she shouted rudely. "I'll ruin your stupid old contest. How dare you lock up my forklift trucks. You're a rotten mean old pig!"

"Ermyntrude," said the king sternly, putting down his tapestry, "you will do as you are told." And he got up and left the royal tearoom.

Princess Ermyntrude was very, very angry. She bent the toasting fork in half and stamped on the bread.

"Stupid, stupid, stupid," she said crossly. And she went away to think out a plan.

The first contest to find a prince to marry the Princess Ermyntrude took place the next day. The king had beamed a message by satellite to all the neighboring countries, and helicopters with eligible princes in them were arriving in dozens at the palace heliport.

The princess watched them from the window of her room, where she was sulking.

"Stupid, stupid," she said. "Why, not one of them even pilots his own helicopter."

And she went on sulking.

After lunch, the king sent a messenger to announce that the princess was to dress in her best robes and come to the great hall of the palace.

She put on her golden dress and her fur cape and her small golden crown and her large golden shoes (for she had big feet) and down she went.

At the door of the throne room she stopped to give the herald time to announce her name, then she went in.

Seated inside were seventy-two princes, all seeking her hand in marriage.

The princess looked at them all. They all looked back.

"Sit here, my dear," said the king loudly, and under his breath, he added, "and behave yourself!"

The princess said nothing.

"Good afternoon and welcome to you all," began the king. "We are here today to find a suitable husband for the lovely Princess Ermyntrude, my daughter. The first competition in this contest will be that of height. As you know, the princess is a very tall girl. She cannot have a husband shorter than herself so you will all line up while the Lord Chamberlain measures you."

The seventy-two princes lined up in six rows and the Lord Chamberlain took out the royal tape measure and began to measure them.

"Why can't I have a shorter husband?" whispered the princess.

"Be quiet. You just can't," said the king.

"Forty-eight princes left in the contest, Your Majesty," cried the Lord Chamberlain.

"Thank you," said the king. "I'm sorry you gentlemen had a wasted journey but you are welcome at the banquet this evening."

And he bowed very low.

"The second competition," said the king, "will be that of disposition. The Princess Ermyntrude has a beautiful disposition, none better, but she does have a slightly hasty temper. She cannot have a husband who cannot match her temper. So we shall have a face-pulling, insult-throwing contest. The Lord Chamberlain will call your names one by one and you will come forward and confront the princess, pull the worst face you can manage, put on a temper display, and insult her."

"Your Majesty, is this wise? Twenty-four of the princes have retired in confusion already," hissed the Lord Chamberlain.

"Weaklings," murmured the princess sweetly.

The first prince stepped forward. The Princess Ermyntrude pulled a repulsive face and he burst into tears.

"Eliminated," said the Lord Chamberlain, running forward with a box of tissues. "Next!"

The next and the next after him and the prince following *them* were all eliminated and it was not until the fifth competitor crossed his eyes, stuck out his tongue, and shouted, "Silly crybaby," at the princess, making her so angry that she forgot to shout back, that anyone succeeded at all.

The fifth prince inspired the next four after him but the princes after that were no match for Princess Ermyntrude until the eighteenth and nineteenth princes called her, "Crow face" and "Squiggle bum" and made her giggle.

By the end of the contest, there were seven princes left, all taller and more insulting than the princess.

"And now," said the king, "for the third and final contest. The third competition," he continued, "will be that of strength. As you may know, the Princess Ermyntrude is very strong. She cannot have a weaker husband so you will all line up and wrestle with her."

"Why can't I have a weaker husband?" whispered the princess.

"Be quiet. You just can't," said the king.

So the Lord Chamberlain lined up the seven princes and just as they were being given their instructions the princess, who was flexing her arm muscles, glanced over at the watching crowd of commoners and noticed a short man covered in helicopter engine oil standing at the back. Because she was so tall, Princess Ermyntrude could see him clearly and, as she looked, he looked back at her and winked quite distinctly. The princess looked again. The short man winked again.

"*Helicopter* engine oil!" thought the princess. "That's the sort of man I like."

Just then the short man looked at her and, forming his mouth carefully, whispered silently, "Choose the seventh. Don't beat him."

The princess felt strangely excited. She looked again. The little man pointed discreetly to the tall, rather nervous looking prince at the end of the line-up. "That one," he mouthed.

Princess Ermyntrude didn't much like the look of the seventh prince but she did want to please the helicopter mechanic so she nodded discreetly, rolled up her golden sleeves, and stepped forward to take on the first prince.

CRASH! He hit the mat with staggering force.

CRASH, CRASH, CRASH, CRASH, CRASH.

The next five princes followed. The poor seventh prince was looking paler and paler and his knees were beginning to buckle under him. The princess looked quickly at the mechanic, who nodded briefly, then she moved toward the seventh prince. He seized her feebly by the arm.

"Good heavens, I could floor him with one blow," thought the princess, but she didn't. Instead, she let herself go limp and floppy and two seconds later, for the first time in her life, she lay flat on her back on the floor.

The crowd let out a stupendous cheer. The king and the Lord Chamberlain rushed forward and seized the hands of the young prince.

The poor prince looked very pale.

"This is terrible, terrible," he muttered desperately.

"Nonsense," cried the king. "I award you the hand of the princess and half my kingdom."

"But, Sire . . ." stammered the prince. "I can't."

"Can't!" shouted the king. "What do you mean can't. You can and you will or I'll have you beheaded!"

There was a scuffle in the crowd and the helicopter mechanic darted forward and bent low at the king's feet.

"Majesty," he murmured reverently, "Majesty. I am the prince's helicopter pilot, mechanic, and aide. Prince Florizel is overcome with shock and gratitude. Is that not so, Sire?" he asked, turning to the prince.

"Um, yes, yes, that's right," said the prince nervously.

The mechanic smiled.

"Prince Florizel, of course,

must have the blessing of *his* father, the King of Buzzaramia, whose kingdom adjoins your own, before the ceremony can take place. Is that not so, Sire?"

"Definitely," said the prince.

"Quite, quite," said the king, "I favor these old customs myself. The princess will fly there tomorrow to meet him, in her own royal helicopter."

"And I shall pilot myself," said the princess.

"We shan't go into *that* now," said the king. "Here, you may kiss the princess."

With a small sigh, the prince fainted dead away.

"Shock," said the pilot hastily. "Clearly shock, Your Majesty. It's not every day he wins the hand of such a beautiful, charming, and talented young lady."

And he looked deep into the princess's eyes.

The prince was carried out to his helicopter and flown off by his pilot, with instructions that the Princess Ermyntrude would fly in the following day.

The rest of the contestants and the princess had a large and elegant banquet with an six-meter chocolate cake in the shape of a heart, and liters of ice cream.

"Who made that heart?" asked Ermyntrude.

"I ordered it from Cook," said the king.

"Well, *I* think it's soppy. A heart!" said the princess in disgust.

Next morning she was up early and, dressed in her frog-green flying suit and bright red aviator goggles, she slipped out to the helicopter before the king was up, climbed in and was just warming up the engine when the Lord Chamberlain came rushing out into the garden.

"Stop, stop," he cried, waving his arms wildly. "Stop. His Majesty, your father, is coming too."

The Princess Ermyntrude turned off the master switch and leaned out of the window.

"Well, he'd better hurry and I'm piloting," she said carelessly. "I'll wait three minutes and I'm going if he hasn't come by then."

The Lord Chamberlain rushed into the palace and returned with the king hastily pulling his ermine robe over his nightshirt and replacing his nightcap with a crown.

"You're a dreadful girl, Ermyntrude," he said sadly. "Here I am with a hangover from the chocolate cake and you insist on being selfish."

"I'm *not* selfish," said Ermyntrude. "I'm by far the best pilot in the palace and it's your own fault you've got a hangover if you will encourage Cook to put rum in the chocolate cake. Anyway, all this was your idea. I'm not marrying that silly prince and I'm flying over to tell him so."

"Ermyntrude," cried the King, scandalized. "How can you do such a thing? I'll be ruined. He won the contest. And besides, you've got to marry someone."

"I haven't and I won't," said the princess firmly, and she set the rotor blades in action.

Within an hour, they were flying into the next kingdom and soon they could see the palace shining golden on the highest hilltop.

"Over there," said the king mournfully. "Please change your mind, Ermyntrude."

"Never," said the princess positively. "Never, never, never, never, never."

Below them they could see the landing pad with ostrich feathers and fairy-lights along the strip.

Princess Ermyntrude settled the helicopter gently on the ground, waited for the blades to stop turning, and got out.

The prince's mechanic was standing on the tarmac.

"A perfect landing," he cried admiringly.

The Princess Ermyntrude smiled. Just then, an older man in ermine-trimmed pajamas came running across the grass.

"Florizel, Florizel, what is all this?" he cried.

The mechanic picked up an oil can from beside his feet.

"Put that down, you ninny," cried the man in ermine pajamas. "Don't you know this is a royal princess?"

"You're being ridiculous, Father," said the mechanic. "Of course I know she's a princess. I'm going to marry her."

"*You* are?" cried Princess Ermyntrude's father. "My daughter's not marrying you. She's marrying your prince."

"I am marrying him," said the Princess Ermyntrude.

"She certainly is," said the mechanic. "And in case you're wondering, I *am* Prince Florizel. The other one was an imposter."

"But how?" asked the princess.

"Well," said Prince Florizel, "it was all my father's idea that I should go so I persuaded my mechanic to change places with me. I thought my father would never find out. Then, when I saw the Princess Ermyntrude, I fell instantly in love with her. She had axle grease on her neck and she was so big and strong. Then I realized it was lucky I'd changed places or you'd have eliminated me on height."

"That's right. You're too short," said the king.

"He's not," said the princess.

"No, I'm not, I'm exactly right and so is she," said Prince Florizel. "Then, when I saw her making faces and shouting insults and throwing princes to the ground, I knew she was the one person I could fall in love with."

"Really?" asked the princess.

"Truly," said Prince Florizel. "Now, come and see my mechanical digger."

And holding the oil can in one hand and the princess's hand in the other, he led the way to the machine shed.

The king looked at Prince Florizel's father.

"There's nothing I can do with her once she's made up her mind," he said wearily.

"I have the same trouble with Florizel," said the second king. "I say, would you like an Alka Seltzer and some breakfast?"

"Would I?" said the princess's father. "I certainly would."

So arm-in-arm they went off together to the palace.

And so Princess Ermyntrude and Prince Florizel were married in tremendous splendor.

The Princess Ermyntrude had a special diamond and gold thread boiler suit made for the wedding and she drove herself to the church in a beautiful bright red forklift truck with E in flashing lights on one side and F picked out in stars on the other and with garlands of flowers on the forks.

Prince Florizel, who had parachuted in for the wedding, wore an emerald and silver thread shirt with silver lamé trousers and had flowers in his beard.

On the steps of the church he reached up on tiptoe to kiss the princess as the television cameras whirred and the people cheered, then they ran down the steps and jumped into the royal forklift and steered away through the excited crowds.

"I'm terribly happy," murmured the prince.

"So am I," said the princess. "I say, did you bring the hamburgers and the ketchup?"

"All there in the back," said the prince.

"And I remembered the wedding cake. Look at it," said the princess proudly.

"Good heavens," cried Prince Florizel. "It's magnificent."

For the wedding cake was shaped like a giant oil can.

"Perfect, don't you think?" murmured the princess.

"Absolutely," said the prince.

And they both lived happily ever after.

THE TERRIBLY PLAIN PRINCESS

Pamela Oldfield

Once upon a time there was this terribly plain Princess. I won't beat about the bush—she was terribly plain. All the visitors at the Royal Christening remarked upon it.

"How extraordinarily plain she is," said her aunt as she handed over a solid silver spoon as a christening present.

"Quite exceptionally so," said her cousin-once-removed as she put a solid gold napkin ring into the Princess's tiny hands.

I say tiny hands, but her hands were a great deal larger than those of most Royal Princesses. Her mouth was wider, too, and her nose was hopelessly snubbed. She also had twenty-three freckles over her nose and cheeks.

The King and Queen watched anxiously as the pile of presents grew higher and the comments on the Princess's plainness grew franker. Finally, the Lord High Chamberlain presented the child with a portrait of himself wearing his full robes of office.

"We shall be hard put to find her a husband," he said gloomily, shaking his head with the worry of it all. The poor Queen could bear it no longer. She burst into tears and sobbed all over the King's best ermine cloak, which did it no good.

The Princess, whose name was Sophia, lived on an island with her mother, Good Queen Matilda, and her father, Good King Ferdinand. The island was the Island of Toow and was one of a group of islands with original names like the Island of Wun and the Island of Thri. Farther over to the right was the Island of Faw but nobody talked about that one. It was uninhabited and a bit of an eyesore, with trees and wildflowers all over the place and no street lighting. All the islands were surrounded by seas of an incredible blue and a golden sun shone all the time.

The terribly plain Princess thrived in this beautiful kingdom, but any hopes that she might grow out of her plainness faded with the passing of the years. She didn't look like a Princess and she didn't behave like one. Sometimes her Royal cousins from Thri and Wun would come over to visit. They would play very genteel games, like "The farmer's in his Royal den," and "Here we go gathering Royal nuts in May," but the Princess Sophia was bored by it all. She would slip away to find Bert, the gardener's boy. He was her one and only true best friend in all the world—or so she told him.

Bert was also terribly plain. He had a snub nose, large hands, a wide mouth, and twenty-eight freckles. He worked very hard because the gardener was bone idle and spent most of his time sleeping in a wheelbarrow in the shade of a Royal pear tree.

Bert trimmed the hedges and weeded the paths and raked the leaves off the grass. When Bert wasn't working in the gardens he was busy with his secret plan to grow a giant blue marigold. He confided this secret to no one but the Princess Sophia—and the cook and most of his relations (and he came from a very large family).

The Princess loved to help him, and together they mixed powders to sprinkle and solutions to spray. They grew a giant orange marigold and some small blue marigolds but never a giant blue one. It was very disappointing for Bert but he was a sunny sort of boy and he refused to give up hope.

When the terribly plain Princess was fifteen, Good King Ferdinand sent for the Lord High Chamberlain.

"Look here," he said, "what are you doing about finding a husband for the Princess Sophia?"

The Lord High Chamberlain bowed low.

"Everything is in hand, Your Majesty," he said proudly. "I think I may say in all modesty, and without fear of contradiction, though I say it myself as shouldn't—"

"Get on with it, man," said the King. It was rather unkingly of him but his nerves were frayed by sleepless nights spent worrying about his daughter's future.

The Lord High Chamberlain tried again. "Bearing in mind the Princess Sophia's terrible plainness of face and largeness of hands, I have now discovered the ideal husband for your daughter."

The King sighed.

"I suppose he, too, is terribly plain," he said.

"On the contrary, Your Majesty, Prince Archibald is of Royal and noble countenance."

The King began to feel much happier.

"And where does this Prince live?" he asked.

"On the Island of Ayte," said the Lord High Chamberlain.

The King lowered his voice to a whisper.

"And what is it that makes the Prince an ideal husband for the Princess Sophia?" he asked.

The Lord High Chamberlain lowered his voice also.

"Your Majesty," he said, "the Prince Archibald is terribly short-sighted—in a Royal sort of way. I doubt if he will notice that his bride is terribly plain."

Good King Ferdinand was delighted. He told Good Queen Matilda, who was delighted, and together they told the Princess Sophia, who was horrified.

"But I don't want to marry him," she protested, and she stamped her foot and looked plainer than ever. "I want to marry Bert, the gardener's boy, and help him grow a giant blue marigold."

"But, dearest child," said her mother, "the gardener's boy is terribly plain and Prince Archibald is of Royal and noble countenance."

"Royal and noble poppycock!" said the Princess. "I want to marry Bert."

But her protestations went unheeded and the date was set for the wedding. You may well be wondering what Bert had to say about all this. The fact is that he didn't say anything because he had designed a square parasol to shelter the marigolds from the sun's rays at midday and was trying to decide the best position for it.

On the Island of Ayte, Prince Archibald was not looking forward to his coming betrothal either, because he was a confirmed bookworm. His rooms in the palace had books where books should be and books where books shouldn't be. Scattered among the books were various pairs of spectacles to help him with his reading. (There were times when his parents worried about him.)

The day of the Royal wedding dawned bright and clear. The Royal party set sail from the Island of Ayte in the Good Ship *Aytee*, bound for the Island of Toow.

The Princess Sophia waited on the quayside with Good King Ferdinand and Good Queen Matilda and the Lord High Chamberlain and hundreds of lesser mortals. The terribly plain Princess wore a beautiful gown of white and gold lace and a rather thick veil. As the Prince's ship drew alongside the quay a great cheer went up from the Princess's supporters and the Prince put down his book and went up on deck. It was a proud moment for the people of Toow when the Prince Archibald, of Royal and noble countenance, prepared to meet the terribly plain Princess Sophia.

But it was not to be. It so happened that the Prince Archibald had forgotten to take off his reading spectacles and put on his walking-about spectacles. Instead of stepping onto the ship's gangplank he missed it by a good few inches and stepped straight into the incredibly blue sea!

Now, although the people of Toow were nice, well-mannered people, it isn't every day you can see a Royal Prince plopping into the water like that. I have to admit that they all fell about laughing. Some of them laughed so much that *they* fell into the water as well.

Poor Prince Archibald was very upset. As soon as he was fished out of the water he gave orders to sail back to Ayte and turned to the next chapter in his book. The terribly plain Princess Sophia was also upset. She ran away to find Bert and weep on his shoulder, but when she did find him he was at the top of a stepladder, adjusting the square parasol over his precious marigold plants. The Princess fell to her knees on the grass below him, and wept terribly plain tears all over the marigolds.

When Bert came down five minutes later to see what was going on he could hardly believe his eyes. The marigolds were beginning to grow! The plants grew taller and taller and produced giant buds that burst into bloom. Yes! You've guessed it. Bright blue marigolds!

That's almost the end of the story. Bert was awarded a medal—the Gardener's Silver Cross—and he was allowed to marry the Princess. They went to live on the Island of Faw, where they raised many new and wonderful plants with the help of Princess Sophia's terribly plain tears. (She could cry to order by thinking how nearly she had married the Prince Archibald!) Oh yes! They also raised a large family of happy, but terribly plain, children!

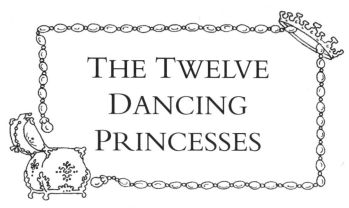

THE TWELVE DANCING PRINCESSES

Brothers Grimm
Retold by Fiona Waters

The King was distracted. His twelve daughters, whom he loved above all the riches in his kingdom, were vexing him greatly. Each one was as beautiful as the moon and the stars, and the King had thought that his only anxiety would be to find twelve young princes fine enough to be their husbands. But now the King had a far greater worry. Every morning at breakfast the Princesses would appear, looking as if they hadn't slept a wink all night. And they were fit for nothing all day. They yawned through investitures, they fell asleep during presentations by the foreign ambassadors, and worst of all, they were not looking their best for the official court portrait painter. An even greater mystery was that their shoes were worn through entirely.

In the end, after telling the Princesses off more times than he could remember, the King resorted to stronger measures. Every evening he would kiss each of his daughters good night, then the Queen would lock their bedroom door securely and put the key around her neck on a golden chain. But in the morning there were the worn-out shoes and the yawning Princesses. So how did they get out? And where did they go? The Princesses were not telling. They just smiled—when they were not asleep, that is.

The King was determined to solve the mystery. Aside from his worry over his daughters' future prospects, their shoes were costing a fortune. The King sent court messengers to all four corners of his kingdom with the proclamation that he would give the hand of one of the Princesses in marriage to the man who could discover the secret of where they went every night. But should he fail after three attempts, he would be banished forever.

There was, of course, a great stream of young men willing to risk banishment for such a wondrous prize. Dukes and counts, generals and admirals, mayors and doctors—all came flocking to the palace. But every single one failed in the task. Before the Princesses retired for the night they would sing and play their musical instruments and feed each suitor sweetmeats and rich honeyed mead. The next thing the young man knew, morning had come and there were the sleepy Princesses and twelve pairs of worn-out shoes. Only the court shoemaker went around with a smile on his face. Never before had business been so good.

One day a handsome but penniless young soldier wandered back into the kingdom after a long campaign far away in foreign lands. He read the King's proclamation and decided to try his luck. As he sat bathing his feet in a stream an old woman came slowly down the dusty road. The young man offered her some of his bread and cheese, and as they sat contentedly together the old woman asked where he was bound. When he told her he was going to the palace, she said, "Well, I might be able to help you. Those wily Princesses will offer you a goblet of honeyed mead. You must not drink a single drop, for it is drugged. Pretend to be asleep, and you shall see what you shall see. Now, I have a gift for you to thank you for sharing your food with me." The old woman handed him a soft, silvery cloak. "This is a cloak of invisibility. Use it well!" And with a quick smile the old woman disappeared, as if by magic.

The young soldier set off for the palace, the cloak tucked safely in his knapsack. When he arrived, the court was in uproar. The King was tearing his hair out. The court shoemaker had taken on extra cobblers to help keep up with the demand for new shoes every day, and his bills were becoming quite astronomical. The Princesses were dozing over their bowls of porridge at breakfast as usual, and their governess despaired of managing to keep them awake long enough to teach them anything.

The young soldier bowed deeply to the King and looked at the Princesses. They were all so beautiful, especially the youngest. As she smiled at him he determined to succeed in solving the mystery and so win her hand in marriage. That evening he ate a hearty supper, but when the eldest Princess gave him a goblet of honeyed mead, he only pretended to drink it.

A couch was placed behind a wooden screen just inside the door of the Princesses' bedroom. The King and Queen came to kiss the Princesses good night. As he passed by the young man, the King hissed in his ear, "Do not fail me! I am relying on you," and he and the Queen swept out of the bedroom, locking the door firmly.

The young man yawned hugely and sank into the cushions on the couch as if he had fallen asleep. The Princesses came over to look at him. He gave a gentle snore. The eldest Princess laughed. "Another poor fool who will never find out our secret! Come, my sisters— it will soon be midnight." And they rushed away with a flurry of skirts, all except the youngest Princess, who paused to look at the young soldier. Truth be told, she was rather taken with his quiet ways and handsome good looks. But then she too turned away.

The room was filled with the sounds of rustling fabric and excited whispers, and after a few minutes the young man cautiously slid off the couch and peeped around the edge of the screen. The room was a hive of activity. The Princesses were all wearing gorgeous velvet and brocade dresses. They giggled as they brushed and pinned up their hair, powdered their faces, and then pulled on the brand-new jeweled slippers that the shoemaker had delivered only a few hours earlier. On went rings and necklaces, and fans and gloves were gathered up as the Princesses flew hither and thither about the room. Then the eldest Princess clapped her hands three times. A trapdoor opened up in the middle of the floor, and they all swiftly went down some steeply curving steps. Just as soon as the youngest Princess had disappeared through the trapdoor, the young man flung the silvery cloak around his shoulders and hurried after them.

The steps wound around and around, deeper and deeper. They were lit by flaring torches. As the young soldier made his way cautiously after the Princesses he could hear their laughter ahead. He felt a warm breeze on his face, and when the steps came to an end, he found himself in a courtyard lit by hundreds of tall, white candles. A sweeping staircase led to a terrace where splashing fountains played amid carved marble statues. Below the terrace lay a wondrous garden where trees covered in rich jewels glittered in the candlelight. Long tables were spread with all manner of delicious food laid out on golden plates, and wine sparkled in silver goblets. Musicians played whirling tunes, and he saw that every one of the Princesses was dancing with a richly dressed and most handsome prince.

The young soldier was spellbound by this secret and enchanted world far beneath the castle, and he gazed around in utter astonishment. But he managed to keep his wits about him. He reached up and broke off a branch from one of the trees and hid it under his cloak. Swiftly he ran back through the garden, across the terrace, up the staircase, through the courtyard, and out of the trapdoor, back into the real world. He put the jeweled branch inside his knapsack and lay down on the couch, looking as if he had never stirred.

As dawn peeped through the curtains he heard the Princesses climb slowly up the steep steps back into their bedroom. The splendid ballgowns went back into the wardrobes; the jewels, fans, and gloves went back into the drawers; and twelve pairs of shoes, worn through entirely with dancing, were kicked off twelve pairs of tired feet. The Princesses climbed into their four-poster beds, drew the curtains, and lay down as if they had not moved all night. When the King unlocked the door, the young man stretched ostentatiously, as if he had just woken up, and merely asked for his breakfast. He refused to meet the King's gaze, so of course everyone assumed that he had not found out the Princesses' secret.

The next night all happened as before, and this time the young man brought back a silver goblet from the garden, and the third night, a golden plate.

It was with a weary voice that the King asked the young soldier at breakfast on the fourth day if he had found out where the Princesses went at night. He sat up very quickly when the young man told his tale and produced first the branch from the tree, then the silver goblet, and finally the golden plate. The King was just delighted, but the Princesses were furious that he had managed to outwit them. Now they would never be able to return to their enchanted princes in their magical world. They looked very cross indeed, all except the youngest, who smiled very sweetly at the young soldier. And, of course, he chose her for his bride.

The King had the enchanted trapdoor bolted shut and a very heavy tasseled carpet laid on top. The Queen arranged a great number of parties after that, so the remaining eleven Princesses met many handsome princes from distant lands, all of whom were very good dancers. It was not long before every single Princess was happily married, and everyone lived contentedly ever after.

Except, of course, the court shoemaker, whose business declined very rapidly. Thereafter he always made the young soldier's boots just a little too tight, so they pinched. . . .

THE SPIDER IN THE BATH

Joan Aiken

Once there was a princess called Emma. Her father the king was a fussy, selfish man, always finding fault with the weather. If there were several hot days together he would grumble, "When in the world is it going to rain?" If the wind blew he said, "I can't stand this tiresome wind," and if it rained he said, "Why doesn't the sun ever shine?"

He was so busy complaining about the weather that he had no time to spare for his daughter, who led a rather glum life. Her mother the queen had died when Emma was only two, and she had nobody to play with. The king would not permit her to play with the palace pages or the prime minister's daughter. Ludo, or dominoes, or Snakes and Ladders with the under-nursemaid were the only games allowed her.

So Emma was often lonely and bored, and, as lonely bored people often do, she had become rather selfish and nasty.

The king's great-grandmother had been a witch, and Emma had a little seed of witchcraft in her —not much, but, as she grew lonelier and nastier, the seed of witchcraft grew bigger.

When she was six, she discovered an interesting thing about herself. She found that if she kept her whole mind very still, and thought very hard indeed, she could move small objects from one place to another without touching them.

For instance, she could move a pea or a potato chip from one side of her plate to the other, just by watching it and thinking about it and willing it to move.

She found this out by accident one day when the palace doctor had come to see her because she had a cold. He took her temperature and shook an aspirin out of a bottle, and was just about to pop it into Emma's mouth when the aspirin rolled out of his hand, fell on the floor, and bounced out of sight under Emma's bed.

"Confound it!" said the doctor, "Where's that pill got to?"

He shook out another aspirin, and that did the same thing.

Emma's face was perfectly straight, but inside she was laughing her head off. After he had lost four aspirins, the doctor, very annoyed, gave the bottle to the under-nursemaid, Hattie, and told her to see that the princess had one before she went to sleep. He had better things to do with his time.

Of course Emma never took an aspirin. She detested medicine. And she could always get her own way with Hattie, who was very shy in her new job, only seven or eight years older than the princess herself, and a little frightened of Emma. With good reason. For soon, Hattie discovered that when Emma's cold blue eyes were on her, pins were likely to drop out of her fingers, or prick her sharply; buttons that she was supposed to be sewing on shirts would roll away and lose themselves; plates would slip from her grasp; or the hairpins would drop, all together, out of her shining hair, and Miss Targe, the head nurse, coming in and seeing Hattie's hair fall over her face, would scold her for untidiness.

Hattie soon began to suspect that the Princess Emma was the cause of these troubles, but how could she be sure? And anyway, there was nothing in the world she could do about it.

When Hattie played Snakes and Ladders with the princess, the dice would be sure to roll over and over, giving the princess nothing but sixes, while Hattie had a steady run of ones and twos. Also, Emma's counters seemed to skip ahead around the board by themselves, even when Emma's hands were nowhere near the table. When they played games, Hattie always lost.

After a while, Emma found that she was able to move large things—oranges and apples and shoes and plates and hairbrushes. It was hard work doing this—she had to squeeze her mind together like a clenched fist inside her head, while sitting completely still, watching the thing she was trying to move. She had to hold her breath and almost stop her heart from beating. The first time she managed to roll an orange from one end of the breakfast table to the other she felt so tired that she had to go and lie down on her bed for half an hour.

But soon she grew better at her strange game. One day she even managed to move an apple right through the wall, from the nursery into her bedroom next door. Moreover the apple went clean through the plaster without even leaving a hole! How about that! Emma was so proud of what she had done that she wanted to dance around the room and shout—but there was nobody whom she could tell.

The king her father would have said, "Quiet, please, Emma. Princesses should be seen and not heard," and then gone on grumbling about the weather. Hattie would have been scared to death, and worried as well. The palace pages would snigger disbelievingly. And the head nurse, Miss Targe, would say, "That's quite enough of that, Your Highness. We don't want such goings-on in our nurseries. Now go and wash your hands."

So Emma went on practicing by herself, in secret.

She moved a tooth out of her father's head, just before he bit into a piece of toast. She moved Hattie's fur bonnet onto the fire, one snowy afternoon, so the poor girl had to take Emma for a walk without it, and caught a nasty cold. Emma moved a rosebush into the middle of the palace lawn, greatly annoying the head gardener, who wondered for the rest of his life how it had happened. She moved a shoe from the hoof of one of the horses pulling the royal carriage, and a rolling pin from the cook's hand into the oven.

Sometimes Emma's trick went wrong.

You know how, if someone knocks your elbow when you are pouring milk into a cup, the milk splashes all over the table. If some sudden sight or sound startled Emma when she was concentrating on moving an object, the result was rather queer.

The first time it happened was at lunch, when the footman set a dish of strawberries in front of the king. Emma fixed her mind on the dish, intending to move it just out of her father's reach, but a speck of dust on her nose made her sneeze, and instead of sliding away, the plate of berries shook and quivered and splintered and split up—so that suddenly, instead of just one dish, there were a hundred identical blue bowls, each full of red strawberries, lined up before the king in ten rows of ten.

He was furious, of course.

"Is this supposed to be some sort of joke?" he roared, and dismissed the cook, the butler, and all the footmen.

Emma wasn't in the least sorry for the people who had been sacked, just interested in what had gone wrong with her magic.

The same thing happened on a day when she was trying to move a narrow gold ring off Hattie's little finger. The ring had been left to Hattie by her mother when she died, and this annoyed Emma, whose own mother had left her nothing but a crown, which she would not be allowed to wear until she grew up. But the ring, a child's ring, very tiny, was tight on Hattie's finger, and in struggling to shift it, Emma's mind must have lost its grip for a second. The result was a hundred little gold rings glittering and clinking in the bathroom basin, which Hattie was doing her best to polish.

"My goodness gracious, Your Highness!" Hattie exclaimed. "Where ever in the world did all these rings come from?"

"Never mind where they came from. You'd better have them," said Emma crossly. "They are yours, in a way."

"No, indeed they are not, Your Highness." And Hattie carried them to Miss Targe, who scolded her, and whisked up the rings in her apron, saying they must have been left behind by a burglar. She took them to the palace security officer, who sold them and kept the money.

Still, apart from a few accidents like these, Emma, by regular practice, became more and more skillful at moving objects. By the time she reached her teens, she was growing ambitious and wanted to move live creatures. Think of moving a tiger out of the royal zoo! Or her father off his throne, down into the middle of the palace lily pond!

Emma found that moving live things was much harder work. She had to practice on very small creatures first, fruit flies, and the ants that ran over the palace terrace. Even houseflies were too large and fidgety. Bees, wasps, and bumblebees were too big, and their buzzing gave Emma pins and needles in her mind.

She still hadn't gone beyond ants when, one night, as she was getting ready for bed, she found a spider in her marble bath.

Emma detested spiders. And this was a particularly big one, black and furry and bunchy and long-legged. He kept very still indeed, but when he did move, when Emma's shadow fell across the bath, it was with such a sudden scurrying scuttle that Emma would not have dared touch him for anything in the world. She tried to move him with her mind; but he was much too big for that.

"Hattie!" Emma called loudly. "Miss Targe! Hattie! Come here quickly!"

But Hattie was out, for it was her evening off, and Miss Targe was downstairs having her supper.

Emma had to go to bed without taking a bath.

Next morning the spider was still there. He seemed to have grown a bit bigger.

"Hattie, take the spider out of the bath," said the princess, when the under-nursemaid came in to lay out Emma's clean clothes for the day.

Hattie trembled a little—she was afraid of spiders too—but she carefully and gently wrapped the spider in a cloth-of-silver face towel and shook him out of the window onto the wisteria vine that grew outside.

"Now give the bath a good scrub before I get into it," said Emma.

At breakfast that day, among the mail, there was a letter from the crown prince of Pliofinland, asking for the Princess Emma's hand in marriage. The king snorted irritably over it.

"Who does he think he is? A miserable little twopenny-halfpenny kingdom like Pliofinland! The prince who marries my daughter must bring a hundred gentlemen-at-arms, each one carrying a two-pound bag of diamonds. They certainly can't manage that in Pliofinland."

And he dictated a letter of refusal to his secretary.

Emma was delighted to think that her father valued her so highly. She spent the day trying to move a wasp out of a jam jar, and finally managed to shift it into a pot of face cream.

A month or so later, the spider was there in the bath again, and he seemed to have grown—to Emma's horrified eyes he appeared about as big as a plum. She tried again to shift him with her mind, but she couldn't.

Hattie was downstairs doing a bit of ironing, and Miss Targe was having her supper, so again Emma went to bed without her bath.

In the morning she ordered Hattie to kill the spider.

"Oh, no, Your Highness, I couldn't!"

"Go on, don't be such a coward!" said Emma crossly.

"It's bad luck to kill spiders, Your Highness!"

In the end, Hattie, trembling like a leaf, wrapped the spider in a golden towel, and carefully put him out of the window among the wisteria leaves.

"Throw him down on the terrace!" ordered the princess. "Otherwise he'll only find his way in again."

But Hattie was too kindhearted to do that. And Emma was secretly angry because Hattie had been brave enough to do something she couldn't do herself.

A few months later, when Emma went to bed, the spider was back in the bath again, and now he was as big as a furry tennis ball with legs.

"Get out, you horrible thing!" said Emma, and she turned on the cold tap. The spider scurried to and fro in the bath, as the water rose. His frantic movements frightened Emma, who thought he might jump right out of the bath. She turned the water off, switched off the light, shut and locked the bathroom door, and, without washing or brushing her teeth, jumped into bed, knocking over a glass of water on the bedside table. She hid her head under the covers, furious with the spider for having frightened her so.

"In the morning I'm going to move him," she decided angrily.

For that same day, at her practice, she had managed to move a canary chick and a small dormouse provided by the palace gardener.

"If I can move a mouse, I can move a spider," thought Emma. "I'll show him who's master."

So, next morning, when it was light and she felt braver, Emma put on her ermine dressing gown and went into the bathroom, filled with determination.

There sat the spider, and he had grown in the night. Now he was as big and hairy as a coconut.

Emma heard Hattie come into her bedroom with an armful of clean clothes.

"Now," she thought, "I must do it quickly!" and she focused her mind on the spider like a gardener turning on a jet of hose water.

But just at that moment Hattie cut her finger on a piece of broken glass that Emma had knocked over and left where it lay.

Hattie let out a sharp cry of pain, and Emma's mind was jolted off its track. The spider in the bath jerked—quivered—shivered—fell apart —and, all of a sudden, instead of just one,

there were a hundred huge black furry spiders,
filling the bath to the brim, jostling and rustling and
staring hard at Emma with their beady black eyes.

Emma let out a screech, which brought Hattie
running with a handkerchief bundled around her
bleeding finger. Hattie herself was so horrified by
the sight of what was in the tub that she could
only gasp, "*Oh!* Your Highness!"

"This was *your* fault," said Emma savagely. "So
now *you* can get rid of them! Go on—that's an
order."

She was furious that she had failed to move the
spider.

Hattie, white as cotton wool, stepped toward the
towel rail, but Emma shouted, "No! You are to take
those spiders out of the bath with your hands.
I don't want those spiders touching my towel.
Go on! Take them in your hands and drop them
out of the window."

"Oh, Your Highness! You wouldn't make me do that!"

"Wouldn't I just!" said Emma. "Do it, or you're fired, and I'll see that you get sent to jail for disobeying my orders."

So Hattie, her teeth chattering with terror, crept to the bath, and plunged her hands to the wrists into the heaving furry mass of spiders. Her finger was still dripping blood.

"Well, one good thing," thought Hattie, "they do say a cobweb's the best plaster to put on a cut." So that cheered her up a little.

She picked up a double handful of spiders, all tangled together, and then, with her eyes shut, ran across to the window and dropped them out.

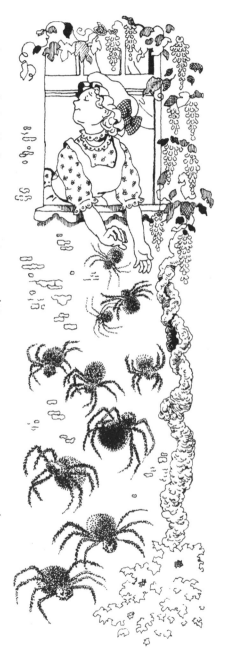

Down they slid, on thick, silvery webs, and left her hands all coated in web too, like gray silk gloves.

"Hurry up!" said Emma. "Don't stop. Get rid of them all!"

To and fro, to and fro Hattie went, with armful after armful of spiders. By the time she had carried half a dozen loads of the black furry creatures, she found she didn't mind them quite so much. And presently she began to feel quite friendly toward them. After all, they were soft as thistledown, and they didn't bite, or sting, or even struggle, but just quietly let her carry them. Hattie, for her part, took tremendous care not to bruise them or bend their legs or bump them against each other, and she let each one glide gently down on its own web onto the terrace below.

There were exactly a hundred.

As she let out the last one—"Oh, my goodness gracious!" cried Hattie. "Oh, my word, Your Highness, do come and look!"

But Emma had flounced into the bathroom and was crossly brushing her teeth and didn't hear Hattie's cry of wonder.

Down below on the terrace, instead of a hundred spiders, there were a hundred handsome young men, all bowing and smiling. One of them had a crown on his head and a knapsack on his back, the rest carried plastic bags of diamonds.

They all gazed up admiringly at Hattie's pink cheeks, blue print dress, and shining golden hair. The one who wore the crown bowed particularly low, and gave Hattie an especially warm smile. Even pinker than usual, she smiled shyly back.

"Who in the world are you all?" she asked.

"I'm Prince Boris of Voltolydia," replied the crowned one. "I was on my way here last year to ask for the princess's hand in marriage when my horse had the ill luck to tread on a snake who was a witch in disguise; and she turned me into a spider. She told me I could only be changed back by somebody who was brave enough to pick me up with their bare hands and kind enough to give me a little of their blood."

Hattie looked down at her bare hands, from which the silvery webs were peeling, and noticed with surprise that her cut finger was completely healed, although it had been quite a bad cut.

"So," went on Prince Boris, "I am ever so grateful to you, dear and beautiful girl, for rescuing me, and I should like to ask for your hand in marriage."

"Oh!" said Hattie, blushing even more. "But I'm not the princess, I am only her maid."

"That," said the prince, "makes no difference at all. You are the lady for me. Will you ride back with me and be Queen of Voltolydia?"

"Yes, thank you!" said Hattie, for she had fallen in love with him at first sight, as he had with her. So she pulled up the sash a bit further, stepped out of the window, and slid down the silvery rope of spider-webs, which was easily thick enough to support her.

"Who are all these other young gentlemen?" she asked, looking around at the handsome young men with their bags of diamonds.

"I have no idea," answered Prince Boris. "For some reason they all came and joined me in the bath."

"We wish to be your followers," chorused the young men.

"Certainly you may, if that is your wish," said the prince. "But you might as well leave all these diamonds here. We have enough diamonds in the mines of Voltolydia to keep the  whole world supplied. I brought a bag to offer the princess—but what a disagreeable girl she is. I'm certainly glad that I was saved from marrying *her*!"

Boris and Hattie and all the followers jumped gaily off the palace terrace and hurried away to buy a hundred and one horses to carry them back to Voltolydia—where they lived happily ever after.

All that Princess Emma saw, when she had brushed her teeth and shouted angrily, several times, for Hattie to come and clean the bath, was a wide-open window. When she looked out she noticed, down below, a great many bags of diamonds.

No other prince ever came to ask for Emma's hand. Perhaps word had gotten around how disagreeable she was. She spent the rest of her life moving objects with her mind—larger and larger ones, until at last she was able to move whole cathedrals and power stations and icebergs and moderate-sized mountains.

At first she found it quite an interesting hobby, but in the end she became bored with it, and used to sit for days and days at a time on her throne (for by then the king had died and she had become queen) doing nothing at all whatsoever.

THE SEVENTH
PRINCESS

Eleanor Farjeon

Did you ever hear the tale of the Six Princesses
who lived for the sake of their hair alone?
This is it.

There was once a King who married a gypsy,
and was as careful of her as if she had been made of
glass. In case she ran away he put her in a palace in
a park with a railing all around it, and never let her
go outside. The Queen was too loving to tell him
how much she longed to go beyond the railing,
but she sat for hours on the palace roof, looking
toward the meadows to the east, the river to the
south, the hills to the west, and the markets to
the north.

In time the Queen bore the King twin
daughters as bright as the sunrise, and on the day
they were christened the King, in his joy, asked
what she would have for a gift. The Queen looked

95

from her roof to the east, saw May on the meadows, and said: "Give me the Spring!"

The King called fifty thousand gardeners, and bade each one bring in a root of wildflowers or a tender birch tree from outside, and plant it within the railing. When it was done he walked with the Queen in the flowery park, and showed her everything, saying: "Dear wife, the Spring is yours."

But the Queen only sighed.

The following year two more Princesses, as fair as the morning, were born, and once again, on their christening day, the King told the Queen to choose a gift. This time she looked from the roof to the south, and, seeing the water shining in the valley, said: "Give me the river!"

The King summoned fifty thousand workmen and told them to conduct the river into the park that it should supply a most beautiful fountain in the Queen's pleasure grounds.

Then he led his wife to the spot where the fountain rose and fell in a marble basin, and said: "You now have the river."

But the Queen only gazed at the captive water rising and falling in its basin, and hung her head.

Next year two more Princesses, as golden as the day, were born, and the Queen, given her choice of a gift, looked north from the roof at the busy town, and said: "Give me the people!"

So the King sent fifty thousand trumpeters down to the marketplace, and before long they returned, bringing six honest market-women with them.

"Here, dear Queen, are the people," said the King.

The Queen secretly wiped her eyes, and then gave her six beautiful babies into the charge of the six buxom women, so that the Princesses had a nurse apiece.

Now in the fourth year the Queen bore only one daughter, a little one, and dark like herself, whereas the King was big and fair.

"What gift will you choose?" said the King, as they stood on the roof on the day of the christening.

The Queen turned her eyes to the west, and saw a wood pigeon and six swans flying over the hills.

"Oh!" cried she. "Give me the birds!"

The King instantly sent fifty thousand fowlers forth to snare the birds. While they were absent the Queen said: "Dear King, my children are in their cots and I am on my throne, but presently the cots will be empty and I shall sit on my throne no more. When that day comes, which of our seven daughters will be Queen in my stead?"

Before the King could answer the fowlers returned with the birds. The King looked from the humble pigeon, with its little round head sunk in soft breast-feathers, to the royal swans with their long white necks, and said: "The Princess with the longest hair shall be Queen."

Then the Queen sent for the six nurses and told them what the King had said. "So remember," she added, "to wash and brush and comb my daughters' hair without neglect, for on you will depend the future Queen."

"And who will wash and brush and comb the hair of the Seventh Princess?" they asked.

"I will do that myself," said the Queen.

Each nurse was exceedingly anxious that her own Princess should be Queen, and every fine day they took the children out into the flowery meadow and washed their hair in the water of the fountain, and spread it in the sun to dry. Then they brushed it and combed it till it shone like yellow silk, and plaited it with ribbons, and decked it with flowers. You never saw such lovely hair as the Princesses had, or so much trouble as the nurses took with it. And wherever the six fair girls went, the six swans went with them.

But the Seventh Princess, the little dark one, never had her hair washed in the fountain. It was kept covered with a red handkerchief, and tended in secret by the Queen as they sat together on the roof and played with the pigeon.

At last the Queen knew that her time had come. So she sent for her daughters, blessed them one by one, and bade the King carry her up to the roof. There she looked from the meadows to the river, from the markets to the hills, and closed her eyes.

Now, hardly had the King done drying his own, when a trumpet sounded at his gate, and a page came running in to say that the Prince of the World had come. So the King threw open his doors, and the Prince of the World came in, followed by his servant. The Prince was all in a cloth of gold, and his mantle was so long that when he stood before the King it spread the whole length of the room, and the plume in his cap was so tall that the tip touched the ceiling. In front of the Prince walked his servant, a young man all in rags.

The King said: "Welcome, Prince of the World!" and held out his hand.

The Prince of the World did not answer; he stood there with his mouth shut and his eyes cast down. But his Ragged Servant said, "Thank you, King of the Country!" And he took the King's hand and shook it heartily.

This surprised the King greatly.

"Cannot the Prince speak for himself?" he asked.

"If he can," said the Ragged Servant, "nobody has ever heard him do so. As you know, it takes all sorts to make the world: those who speak and those who are silent, those who are rich and those who are poor, those who think and those who do, those who look up and those who look down. Now, my master has chosen me for his servant, because between us we make up the world of which he is Prince. For he is rich and I am poor, and he thinks things and I do them, and he looks down and I look up, and he is silent, so I do the talking."

"Why has he come?" asked the King.

"To marry your daughter," said the Ragged Servant, "for it takes all sorts to make a world, and there must be a woman as well as a man."

"No doubt," said the King. "But I have seven daughters. He cannot marry them all."

"He will marry the one that is to be Queen," said the Ragged Servant.

"Let my daughters be sent for," said the King, "for the time is now come to measure the length of their hair."

So the Seven Princesses were summoned before the King. The six fair ones came in with their nurses, and the little dark one came in by herself. The Ragged Servant looked quickly from one to another, but the Prince of the World kept his eyes down and did not look at any of them.

Then the King sent for the court tailor, with his tape measure; and when he came the six fair Princesses shook down their hair till it trailed on the ground behind them.

One by one they had it measured, while the six nurses looked on with pride—for had they not taken just as much care as they could of their darlings' hair? But, alas! As neither more care nor less had been spent upon any of them, it was now discovered that each of the Six Princesses had hair exactly as long as the others.

The Court held up its hands in amazement, the nurses wrung theirs in despair, the King rubbed his crown, the Prince of the World kept his eyes on the ground, and the Ragged Servant looked at the Seventh Princess.

"What shall we do," said the King, "if my youngest daughter's hair is the same length as the rest?"

"I don't think it is, sir," said the Seventh Princess, and her sisters looked anxious as she untied the red handkerchief from her head. And indeed her hair was not the same length as theirs, for it was cropped close to her head, like a boy's.

"Who cut your hair, child?" asked the King.

"My mother, if you please, sir," said the Seventh Princess. "Every day as we sat on the roof she snipped it with her scissors."

"Well, well!" cried the King. "Whichever is meant to be Queen, it isn't you!"

That is the story of the Six Princesses who lived for the sake of their hair alone. They spent the rest of their lives having it washed, brushed, and combed by the nurses, till their locks were as white as their six pet swans.

And the Prince of the World spent the rest of *his* life waiting with his eyes cast down until one of the Princesses should grow the longest hair, and become his Queen. As this never happened, for all I know he is waiting still.

But the Seventh Princess tied on her red handkerchief again, and ran out of the palace to the hills and the river and the meadows and the markets; and the pigeon and the Ragged Servant went with her.

"But," she said, "what will the Prince of the World do without you in the palace?"

"He will have to do the best he can," said the Ragged Servant, "for it takes all sorts to make the world, those that are in and those that are out."

THE SLEEPING BEAUTY IN THE WOOD

Charles Perrault
Retold by Virginia Haviland

Once upon a time a King and Queen were very unhappy because they had no children. As the years passed they grew sadder and sadder.

But at last, after many years, the Queen had a daughter. Everyone rejoiced, and a very fine christening was held for this Princess. She had, for her godmothers, all the fairies to be found in the whole kingdom—which were seven. They were invited in order that each should make her a gift, according to the custom for fairy godmothers. The King and Queen knew that in this way the Princess would grow up with the best qualities anyone could imagine.

After the christening, all the company returned to the King's palace, where a great feast was ready for the fairies. On the table before each of them was a magnificent setting of heavy gold—a spoon, a knife, and a fork, all made of pure gold with a pattern of diamonds and rubies.

As they were sitting down at the table, there came into the hall a very old fairy, who had not been invited. No one had seen her for more than fifty years, so she was believed to be either dead or under a spell.

The King ordered a place set for the old fairy, too, but he could not give her a spoon, knife, and fork of gold, because the pieces had been made for only seven fairies. The old fairy fancied she had been insulted, and growled threats between her teeth.

One of the young fairies, who sat by her, heard how the old fairy grumbled. She feared the old fairy might give the little Princess a bad gift—so, when they rose from the table, she hid behind the hangings. The young fairy wanted to be last to speak, in order to undo, as much as she could, any evil that the old fairy intended.

Now all the fairies began to make their gifts to the Princess. The youngest, for hers, said that the Princess should be the most beautiful person in the world. The next said that she should have the wit of an angel. The third, that she should have charm in everything she did. The fourth, that she should dance gracefully. The fifth, that she should sing like a nightingale. And the sixth, that she should play all kinds of music perfectly.

The old fairy's turn came next. With her head shaking—more with anger than from old age—she said that the Princess would prick her hand with a spindle and die of the wound. This terrible gift made the whole company shudder. They all began to cry.

At this instant, the young fairy came out of her hiding place and said, "Be assured, O King and Queen, that your daughter shall not die. It is true that I cannot undo all of what my elder has just done. The Princess shall indeed prick her hand with a spindle. But instead of dying, she shall fall into a deep sleep, which shall last a hundred years. After a hundred years, a King's son shall come and wake her."

The King, to avoid this bad luck, at once forbade, on pain of death, anyone to spin or even to have a spindle in the house.

Fifteen years later, when the King and Queen were away at one of their country houses, it happened one day that the young princess was running up and down the palace. She climbed from room to room and came finally to the top of the tower. Here there sat spinning a good old woman who had never heard of the King's command against spindles.

"What are you doing there, goody?" asked the Princess.

"I am spinning, my pretty child," said the old woman, who did not know her.

"Oh!" said the Princess. "This is very pretty! How do you do it? Give it to me, so I may see if I can do it, too."

But no sooner had she taken the spindle than it stuck into her hand, and she fell down in a swoon.

The good old woman cried out for help. People came from all sides and threw water on the Princess's face. They loosened her clothes, struck her on the palms of her hands, and rubbed her temples. But nothing would bring her to herself.

Now the King, who had returned, heard the noise and climbed to the tower. He recalled what the fairies had said. Knowing that it must be, he had the Princess carried into the finest room in his palace and laid upon a bed all embroidered with gold and silver.

One would have taken the Princess for a little angel, she was so very beautiful. Her fainting had not taken away the color from her face. Her cheeks and her lips were red. Her eyes were shut, but she was breathing softly. This proved she was not dead. The King commanded the court to let her sleep quietly till her hour of awakening should come.

At this time the good fairy, who had saved the life of the Princess by putting her to sleep for a hundred years, was far away in another kingdom. She learned what had happened from a little dwarf who had boots in which he could go seven leagues in one stride. The fairy left at once for the palace of the Princess. In an hour she was seen arriving, in a fiery chariot drawn by dragons.

The King handed her out of the chariot. She looked about and approved everything he had done. But, as she was very wise, she thought that the Princess, when it was time for her to awaken, would be greatly alarmed at finding herself alone in the palace. So she touched with her wand everything in the palace—the governesses, maids of honor, gentlemen, officers, cooks, errand boys, guards, pages, and footmen. She also touched all the horses in the stables, with their grooms. She touched the great dogs in the stableyard and little Pouffe, the Princess's spaniel, which lay close to her on the bed.

As soon as she had touched them, they all fell asleep. They would not awaken before the Princess needed them. The very spits at the fire, as full as they could be of partridges and pheasants, fell asleep; and the fire, also.

All this was done in a moment, for fairies are not long at their work.

Soon there had grown up all around the park such a vast number of trees, great and small, brambles and thorn bushes, twining one within another, that neither man nor beast could pass through. Nothing could be seen but the very tops of the towers, and those only from a great distance.

At the end of a hundred years, the son of the King then ruling, who was of another family, was out hunting. He was curious about the towers he saw above a great thick wood.

The Prince asked many people about this. Each one answered differently. Some said it was a ruined old castle, haunted by ghosts. Others said that witches had their night meetings there. The most common opinion was that an ogre lived there, who imprisoned all the little children he could catch.

The Prince was at a loss, not knowing what to believe, when a very old man spoke to him: "Many years ago I heard from my father (who had heard my grandfather say it) that there was in this castle a Princess. She was the most beautiful ever seen. She had been put under a spell, and was to sleep there a hundred years—until a King's son should waken her."

The young Prince felt all afire at these words. He went off at once to see if they were true. Scarcely had he advanced toward the thick wood when all the great trees, brambles, and thorn bushes gave way to let him pass. He walked up a long avenue to the castle. To his surprise, none of his people could follow. The trees closed behind him again as soon as he had passed through, but he went boldly on his way. A young Prince in love is always brave.

He came into a great outer court. What he saw there might have frozen the most fearless person with horror. There was a frightful silence. Nothing was to be seen but stretched out bodies of men and animals, all seeming to be dead. He knew, however, by the red faces of the guards, that they were only asleep. Their goblets, in which some drops of wine remained, showed plainly that they had fallen asleep while drinking.

The Prince then crossed a court paved with marble, went up the stairs, and came into the guard chamber. Guards were standing in rows with their guns upon their shoulders, snoring loudly. He went on through several rooms full of gentlemen and ladies, all asleep, some standing, others sitting.

At last the Prince came into a chamber all glittering with gold. Here he saw upon a bed the finest sight he had ever beheld—a Princess, who appeared to be about fifteen years of age, and whose bright beauty had something of heaven in it. He approached with trembling and admiration, and fell down before her upon his knees.

And now, as the enchantment was at an end, the Princess awoke. Looking on the Prince with tender eyes, she said, "Is it you, my Prince? I have waited a long time."

The Prince, charmed with these words, and even more with the manner in which they were spoken, knew not how to show his joy and thanks. He vowed he loved her better than he did himself.

The Prince and Princess talked for four hours together, and yet they said not half of what they had to say.

Meanwhile all the palace awoke. Everyone thought about his own business. And, as they were not all in love, they were dying of hunger.

The chief maid of honor grew very impatient and told the Princess loudly that supper was served.

The Prince then helped the Princess to rise. She was dressed magnificently, and His Royal Highness took care not to tell her she was dressed like his great-grandmother. She looked not a bit the less beautiful for all that.

Into the great hall of mirrors they went to dine. Violins and oboes played old tunes. The music was excellent, though it was now over a hundred years since the instruments had been played.

After supper, without losing any time, the Prince and Princess were married in the chapel of the palace.

In two years, the Prince's father died. The Prince and Princess became the new King and Queen, and were given a royal welcome at the capital.

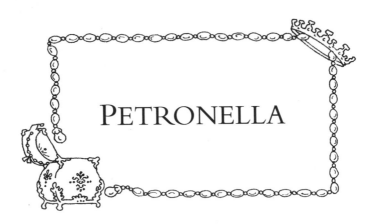

PETRONELLA

Jay Williams

In the kingdom of Skyclear Mountain, three princes were always born to the king and queen. The oldest prince was always called Michael, the middle prince was always called George, and the youngest was always called Peter. When they were grown, they always went out to seek their fortunes. What happened to the oldest prince and the middle prince no one ever knew. But the youngest prince always rescued a princess, brought her home, and in time ruled over the kingdom. That was the way it had always been. And so far as anyone knew, that was the way it would always be.

Until now.

Now was the time of King Peter the twenty-sixth and Queen Blossom. An oldest prince was born, and a middle prince. But the youngest prince turned out to be a girl.

"Well," said the king gloomily, "we can't call her Peter. We'll have to call her Petronella. And what's to be done about it, I'm sure I don't know."

There was nothing to be done. The years passed, and the time came for the princes to go out and seek their fortunes. Michael and George said good-bye to the king and queen and mounted their horses. Then out came Petronella. She was dressed in traveling clothes, with her bag packed and a sword by her side.

"If you think," she said, "that I'm going to sit at home, you are mistaken. I'm going to seek my fortune, too."

"Impossible!" said the king.

"What will people say?" cried the queen.

"Look," said Prince Michael, "be reasonable, Pet. Stay home. Sooner or later a prince will turn up here."

Petronella smiled. She was a tall, handsome girl with flaming red hair and when she smiled in that particular way it meant she was trying to keep her temper.

"I'm going with you," she said. "I'll find a prince if I have to rescue one from something myself. And that's that."

The grooms brought out her horse, she said good-bye to her parents, and away she went behind her two brothers.

They traveled into the flatlands behind Skyclear Mountain. After many days, they entered a great dark forest. They came to a place where the road divided into three, and there at the fork sat a little, wrinkled old man covered with dust and spiderwebs.

Prince Michael said haughtily, "Where do these roads go, old man?"

"The road on the right goes to the city of Gratz," the man replied. "The road in the center goes to the castle of Blitz. The road on the left goes to the house of Albion the enchanter. And that's one."

"What do you mean by 'And that's one'?" asked Prince George.

"I mean," said the old man, "that I am forced to sit on this spot without stirring, and that I must answer one question from each person who passes by. And that's two."

Petronella's kind heart was touched. "Is there anything I can do to help you?" she asked.

The old man sprang to his feet. The dust fell from him in clouds.

"You have already done so," he said. "For that question is the one which releases me. I have sat here for sixty-two years waiting for someone to ask me that." He snapped his fingers with joy. "In return, I will tell you anything you wish to know."

"Where can I find a prince?" Petronella said promptly.

"There is one in the house of Albion the enchanter," the old man answered.

"Ah," said Petronella, "then that is where I am going."

"In that case I will leave you," said her oldest brother. "For I am going to the castle of Blitz to see if I can find my fortune there."

"Good luck," said Prince George. "For I am going to the city of Gratz. I have a feeling my fortune is there."

They embraced her and rode away.

Petronella looked thoughtfully at the old man, who was combing spiderwebs and dust out of his beard. "May I ask you something else?" she said.

"Of course. Anything."

"Suppose I wanted to rescue that prince from the enchanter. How would I go about it? I haven't any experience in such things, you see."

The old man chewed a piece of his beard. "I do not know everything," he said after a moment. "I know that there are three magical secrets which, if you can get them from him, will help you."

"How can I get them?" asked Petronella.

"Offer to work for him. He will set you three tasks, and if you do them you may demand a reward for each. You must ask him for a comb for your hair, a mirror to look into, and a ring for your finger."

"And then?"

"I do not know. I only know that when you rescue the prince, you can use these things to escape from the enchanter."

"It doesn't sound easy," sighed Petronella.

"Nothing we really want is easy," said the old man. "Look at me—I have wanted my freedom, and I've had to wait sixty-two years for it."

Petronella said good-bye to him. She mounted her horse and galloped along the third road.

It ended at a low, rambling house with a red roof. It was a comfortable looking house, surrounded by gardens and stables and trees heavy with fruit.

On the lawn, in an armchair, sat a handsome young man with his eyes closed and his face turned to the sky.

Petronella tied her horse to the gate and walked across the lawn.

"Is this the house of Albion the enchanter?" she said.

The young man blinked up at her in surprise.

"I think so," he said. "Yes, I'm sure it is."

"And who are you?"

The young man yawned and stretched. "I am Prince Ferdinand of Firebright," he replied. "Would you mind stepping aside? I'm trying to get a suntan and you're standing in the way."

Petronella snorted. "You don't sound like much of a prince," she said.

"That's funny," said the young man, closing his eyes. "That's what my father always says."

At that moment the door of the house opened. Out came a man all dressed in black and silver. He was tall and thin, and his eyes were as black as a cloud full of thunder. Petronella knew at once that he must be the enchanter.

He bowed to her politely. "What can I do for you?"

"I wish to work for you," said Petronella boldly.

Albion nodded. "I cannot refuse you," he said. "But I warn you, it will be dangerous. Tonight I will give you a task. If you do it, I will reward you. If you fail, you must die."

Petronella glanced at the prince and sighed. "If I must, I must," she said. "Very well."

That evening they all had dinner together in the enchanter's cozy kitchen. Then Albion took Petronella out to a stone building and unbolted its door. Inside were seven huge black dogs.

"You must watch my hounds all night," said he.

Petronella went in, and Albion closed and locked the door.

At once the hounds began to snarl and bark. They bared their teeth at her. But Petronella was a real princess. She plucked up her courage. Instead of backing away, she went toward the dogs. She began to speak to them in a quiet voice.

They stopped snarling and sniffed at her. She patted their heads.

"I see what it is," she said. "You are lonely here. I will keep you company."

And so all night long, she sat on the floor and talked to the hounds and stroked them. They lay close to her, panting.

In the morning Albion came and let her out. "Ah," said he, "I see that you are brave. If you had run from the dogs, they would have torn you to pieces. Now you may ask for what you want."

"I want a comb for my hair," said Petronella.

The enchanter gave her a comb carved from a piece of black wood.

Prince Ferdinand was sunning himself and working at a crossword puzzle. Petronella said to him in a low voice, "I am doing this for you."

"That's nice," said the prince. "What's 'selfish' in nine letters?"

"You are," snapped Petronella. She went to the enchanter. "I will work for you once more," she said.

That night Albion led her to a stable. Inside were seven huge horses.

"Tonight," he said, "you must watch my steeds."

He went out and locked the door. At once the horses began to rear and neigh. They pawed at her with their iron hooves.

But Petronella was a real princess. She looked closely at them and saw that their coats were rough and their manes and tails full of burrs.

"I see what it is," she said. "You are hungry and dirty."

She brought them as much hay as they could eat, and began to brush them. All night long she fed them and groomed them, and they stood quietly in their stalls.

In the morning Albion let her out. "You are as kind as you are brave," said he. "If you had run from them they would have trampled you under their hooves. What will you have as a reward?"

"I want a mirror to look into," said Petronella.

The enchanter gave her a mirror made of silver.

She looked across the lawn at Prince Ferdinand. He was doing exercises leisurely. He was certainly handsome. She said to the enchanter, "I will work for you once more."

That night Albion led her to a loft above the stables. There, on perches, were seven great hawks.

"Tonight," said he, "you must watch my falcons."

As soon as Petronella was locked in, the hawks began to beat their wings and scream at her.

Petronella laughed. "That is not how birds sing," she said. "Listen."

She began to sing in a sweet voice. The hawks fell silent. All night long she sang to them, and they sat like feathered statues on their perches, listening.

In the morning Albion said, "You are as talented as you are kind and brave. If you had run from them, they would have pecked and clawed you without mercy. What do you want now?"

"I want a ring for my finger," said Petronella.

The enchanter gave her a ring made from a single diamond.

All that day and all that night Petronella slept, for she was very tired. But early the next morning, she crept into Prince Ferdinand's room. He was sound asleep, wearing purple pajamas.

"Wake up," whispered Petronella. "I am going to rescue you."

Ferdinand awoke and stared sleepily at her. "What time is it?"

"Never mind that," said Petronella. "Come on!"

"But I'm so sleepy," Ferdinand objected. "And it's so pleasant here."

Petronella shook her head. "You're not much of a prince," she said grimly. "But you're the best I can do."

She grabbed him by the wrist and dragged him out of bed. She hauled him down the stairs. His horse and hers were in a separate stable, and she saddled them quickly. She gave the prince a shove, and he mounted. She jumped on her own horse, seized the prince's reins, and away they went like the wind.

They had not gone far when they heard a tremendous thumping. Petronella looked back. A dark cloud arose behind them, and beneath it she saw the enchanter. He was running with great strides, faster than the horses could go.

"What shall we do?" she cried.

"Don't ask me," said Prince Ferdinand grumpily. "I'm all shaken to bits by this fast riding."

Petronella desperately pulled out the comb. "The old man said this would help me!" she said. And because she didn't know what else to do with it, she threw the comb on the ground. At once a forest rose up. The trees were so thick that no one could get between them.

Away went Petronella and the prince. But the enchanter turned himself into an ax and began to chop. Right and left he chopped, slashing, and the trees fell before him.

Soon he was through the wood, and once again Petronella heard his footsteps thumping behind.

She reined in the horses. She took out the mirror and threw it on the ground. At once a wide lake spread out behind them, gray and glittering.

Off they went again. But the enchanter sprang into the water, turning himself into a salmon as he did so. He swam across the lake and leaped out of the water on to the other bank. Petronella heard him coming—*thump! thump!*—behind them again.

This time she threw down the ring. It didn't turn into anything, but lay shining on the ground.

The enchanter came running up. And as he jumped over the ring, it opened wide and then snapped up around him. It held his arms tight to his body, in a magical grip from which he could not escape.

"Well," said Prince Ferdinand, "that's the end of him."

Petronella looked at him in annoyance. Then she looked at the enchanter, held fast in the ring.

"Bother!" she said. "I can't leave him here. He'll starve to death."

She got off her horse and went up to him. "If I release you," she said, "will you promise to let the prince go free?"

Albion stared at her in astonishment. "Let him go free?" he said. "What are you talking about? I'm glad to get rid of him."

It was Petronella's turn to look surprised. "I don't understand," she said. "Weren't you holding him prisoner?"

"Certainly not," said Albion. "He came to visit me for a weekend. At the end of it, he said, 'It's so pleasant here, do you mind if I stay on for another day or two?' I'm very polite and I said, 'Of course.' He stayed on, and on, and on. I didn't like to be rude to a guest and I couldn't just kick him out. I don't know what I'd have done if you hadn't dragged him away."

"But then—" said Petronella, "but then—why did you come running after him this way?"

"I wasn't chasing him," said the enchanter. "I was chasing *you*. You are just the girl I've been looking for. You are brave and kind and talented, and beautiful as well."

"Oh," said Petronella. "I see."

"Hmmm," said she. "How do I get this ring off you?"

"Give me a kiss."

She did so. The ring vanished from around Albion and reappeared on Petronella's finger.

"I don't know what my parents will say when I come home with you instead of a prince," she said.

"Let's go and find out, shall we?" said the enchanter cheerfully.

He mounted one horse and Petronella the other. And off they trotted, leaving Prince Ferdinand of Firebright to walk home as best he could.

THE PRINCESS WHO MET THE NORTH WIND

Wendy Eyton

There was once a princess who lived in a very cold land. The white mountains reached almost to the sky, and the rivers shone silver as the chain the princess wore around her neck.

The king and queen loved their daughter very much and gave her beautiful presents each birthday, but the time came when she had far too much of everything.

"Not another ruby snowbird's egg!" said the princess crossly, as she opened up her parcels. "I have three already." "Take away these pearls—I have enough to play marbles with."

"But, my child, what *can* we give you?" asked the poor king, wringing his hands. "I've searched high and low to find you something different this year."

"I think," said the princess, "that until you can give me the most beautiful jewels in the world to hang on my necklace, I will forget about birthdays."

And she stamped up to bed, taking no notice of her cake, which was built in the shape of an iceberg. The king shook his head sadly, and gave the pearls to the youngest parlormaid.

That night, as the princess lay sleeping, the north wind began to call and blow around her room at the top of the palace. He blew so fiercely that the heavy clouds rolled away across the sky and the stars shone, clear and bright, into the bedroom. The princess thought it must be daylight and sat up in bed, staring and blinking.

"Come to the window, Princess," sang the north wind, "and I will give you the most beautiful jewels in the world for your necklace."

The princess ran to the window and looked up at the sky, where thousands of stars were twinkling and glistening.

"Oh, how beautiful," she whispered. "If only I could reach them."

"Put on your cloak and shoes and come with me, Princess," said the north wind. And he led her down the stairs, through the palace gates, and up the side of the highest mountain in the kingdom.

The princess was not at all happy on the mountain. Her feet were wet, her hands numb, and all the time the north wind blew so hard that her cloak billowed and swelled. The more she climbed, the farther away the stars seemed to be, twinkling and laughing.

"They are so beautiful," she gasped to the north wind, "but there must be an easier way to reach them."

"Look down, look down," sang the north wind. And the princess stared in surprise, for now the stars were below as well as above her, and the whole night seemed on fire with them.

"I must have the stars for my necklace!" she cried, and began to slide and slither down the mountain, tearing her cloak, and cutting her hands on the rocks.

The princess did not realize that the cold breath of the north wind had frozen the lake below the mountain, and that all she could see was the reflection of the stars from the sky above. She reached the bottom of the mountain, ran to the lake, stretched out her hand for the nearest star, and gave a cry of bitter disappointment.

The north wind blew so hard that the pine trees shivered and the snow fell from their branches onto the princess. She tried to pull her cloak together, but it was badly torn.

"How silly I have been," said the princess, "to think I could capture the stars. And here I am at the bottom of a mountain, frozen and hungry, and miles from home."

As the princess thought of her warm bed, and the birthday tea she had refused to eat, and the kindness of her mother and father, three tears trickled down her nose and chin and hung, frozen, to her silver necklace.

Suddenly the branches of the pine trees stopped shivering, and all was still. A young man appeared at the side of the princess and pointed to the frozen tears, which clung to her necklace, gleaming green, purple, and blue in the Northern Lights.

"I am the Prince of the North Wind," he said, "and I have given you the most beautiful jewels in the world."

He took the princess by the hand and led her back to the palace, where there was much laughter and rejoicing.

THE CAT-KING'S DAUGHTER

Lloyd Alexander

Princess Elena of Ventadorn loved Raimond, Count of Albiclair. However, as much as the two young people had set their hearts on marrying, so King Hugo, father of Elena, had set his against it.

"That lute plucker?" cried Hugo. "That verse scribbler? He should be out hunting, or carousing; or invading the next province, like any self-respecting nobleman. Worse yet, his estates are unspeakably small and his fortune intolerably smaller. In short, the fellow's worthless."

"That's your opinion," said Elena. "Not mine."

"Indeed it is," replied Hugo. "And whose judgment better than the King's?"

"You say that about everything," declared Elena. "Because pickled herrings happen to give you colic, you've forbidden them to all your subjects.

Because holidays bore you, the kingdom has none. You can't abide cats, so you've made it a crime to keep one, to feed one, or even to shelter a kitten."

"So it should be," retorted the King. "Cats! Impudent beasts! They won't fetch or carry. They wave their tails in your face. They stare at you bold as brass, then stick out their tongues, and go to washing themselves."

"I call that clean," said Elena, "hardly criminal."

"Worse than criminal, it's disrespectful," snapped the King. "Disobedient and insolent, like headstrong girls who don't take no for an answer."

So, the more Elena urged his consent to marry Raimond, the more stubbornly the King refused. Instead, he sent word for other suitors properly— and profitably—qualified to present themselves at court; and he locked Princess Elena in her chambers, there to receive them and choose one to be her husband.

Princess Elena matched her father in strength of will; and no sooner was the door bolted after her than she determined to escape and make her way to Raimond as quickly as she could.

137

But her chambers in the North Tower of the palace were too high for her to jump from the casement. Since King Hugo disliked ivy, none grew along the steep walls; and, without a handhold, the stones were too smooth for her to clamber down. Though she pulled the sheets and coverlets from her bed and knotted them together, this makeshift ladder barely reached halfway to the courtyard below. The more she cast about for other means, the more clearly she saw there were none. At last, she threw herself on the couch, crying in rage and frustration.

Then she heard a voice say:

"Princess, why do you weep?"

At her feet sat a tabby cat, honey-colored with dark stripes, thin as a mackerel, every rib showing under her bedraggled coat. Though she looked more used to alleys than palaces, she seemed quite at ease amid the soft carpets and embroidered draperies. Instead of crouching fearfully, she studied the Princess with bold curiosity through emerald eyes much the same hue as those of Elena.

"If I had satin cushions to sleep on," said the cat, "and goosedown quilts, and silken bedspreads, I wouldn't be in such a hurry to leave them."

138

"A cat?" exclaimed the Princess, for a moment forgetting her predicament. "But there are no cats in the palace."

"Well, there is one now," answered the cat, "and my name is Margot." She then explained how she had slipped through the palace gate that morning while the guard was changing.

"But why?" asked Elena. "You must know how my father feels about cats. And here, of all places—"

"Where better?" said Margot. "Who'd expect to find a cat under King Hugo's very nose? I was hoping for a warm cubbyhole to hide in, and a few leftovers from the kitchen. But once inside the palace, I had to dodge so many courtiers, and got so turned around in the hallways and staircases, I was glad for the first open door I came to."

"Poor creature," said Elena, venturing to stroke the cat, "you're hardly more than skin and bones."

"Thanks to your father's decree," said Margot. "Luckily, some people have better sense than to pay it any mind. Now and again, a housewife puts out some scraps or a saucer of milk. For the rest, we forage as best we can. King Hugo hasn't made life easy for a cat."

"Nor a princess," replied Elena, glad for the chance to unburden her heart by telling her troubles to Margot.

After listening attentively to the account, the cat thoughtfully preened her whiskers for several moments, then said:

"We cats won't abide doing what we're forced to do, so I understand your feelings. But I doubt very much you can be made to marry against your will. King Hugo may rant and rave; but, practically speaking, he surely won't tie you hand and foot and drag you by the hair to the wedding ceremony. A bride, kicking and screaming? Hardly flattering for a husband-to-be."

"True," Elena admitted. "But I love Raimond and want him for my husband. How shall I make my father change his mind? What if no one else claimed my hand? I'll make sure they don't! I'll paste a wart on the end of my nose, and paint myself a moustache. That should be discouraging enough."

"Princess," said the cat, "your beauty is too great to hide, no matter what you do."

"I won't eat," said Elena. "I'll starve myself."

"Be sensible," said the cat. "Your father need only wait. Your hunger will soon get the best of you."

"I'm afraid you're right," Elena agreed. "Very well, when these suitors come, I'll refuse to see them. Let them break down the door! I shan't speak a word to them. There's nothing else I can do."

"Yes, there is," said the cat. "What I have in mind might even help us cats as well as you. First, you must do as I ask now. Then, tomorrow, you must stay hidden under the couch. Be warned, however: what happens may bring you joy—or it may break your heart."

Princess Elena could not imagine herself more heartbroken than she was. And so, despite the cat's warning, she willingly agreed. As Margot instructed her, she combed and brushed the cat until the fur was as soft and glistening as her own tresses. Then she draped the cat in one of her silken scarves and tied a necklace of pearls at Margot's waist. She set a diamond bracelet as a crown on Margot's head; and adorned the cat's paws and tail with the finest rings of emeralds, rubies, and sapphires.

Next morning, King Hugo came to order his daughter to make ready for her suitors. But instead of Elena, out of sight beneath the couch, he found Margot, royally attired, comfortably stretched out amid the satin pillows.

"What's this?" roared the King. "What's this cat doing here? Scat! Scat!" He shouted for Elena, but she never stirred. Before the King thought to search the chambers, Margot glanced calmly at him and, in a voice resembling that of Elena, said:

"Father, how is it that you don't recognize your own daughter?"

At this, King Hugo stared speechless and his head began to whirl. Seeing nothing of Princess Elena in the apartments, he could only believe that she had indeed turned into a cat overnight. Then his bewilderment turned to anger and he shook a finger under Margot's nose:

"You've done it on purpose," he cried, "out of sheer stubbornness, to vex and spite me! How you managed it, I don't know. But I command you: turn yourself back again! Immediately!"

"That," said Margot, "will be impossible."

King Hugo then declared he would summon the Royal Physician; or, if need be, scour the kingdom for alchemists, astrologers, midwives, village wonder-workers, whoever might transform her once again into human shape.

"That will be of no use," Margot said. "As you see me now, so shall I always be."

"Wretched girl!" King Hugo cried. "Do you mean to make a fool of me? What king ever had a cat for a daughter!"

"What cat ever had a king for a father?" Margot replied.

This only enraged King Hugo the more; and he swore, cat or no, she would receive her suitors and marry the first who was willing.

And so, when the Court Chamberlain came to announce the arrival of the Duke Golo de Gobino, the King tried to compose himself and put the best face he could on the matter. For Golo, while hardly the cleverest, was the richest nobleman in the kingdom, with a purse as full as his head was empty. His estates lay beside those of the King; he had a fine regiment of cavalry, excellent stables and kennels, and his marriage to Elena would be all King Hugo ever could wish.

However, when Duke Golo saw the bejeweled Margot, his self-satisfied smile vanished, and he stammered in dismay:

"The Princess? She looks rather like a cat!"

"Pay it no mind," King Hugo said. "She's not quite herself today."

"So I see," replied Golo. "Indeed, I never would have recognized her. Whatever happened?"

"Nothing," said King Hugo. "A trivial indisposition, a minor ailment."

"But, Majesty," quavered Golo, "it may be contagious. Suppose I caught it from her. If I take her for my wife, the same could happen to me."

"In your case," said Margot, "it might be an advantage."

"Come now, Golo," the King insisted, "get on with it. She'll make you a fine wife."

"One thing certain," added Margot, "you'll never be troubled with mice."

"Majesty," stammered Golo, "I came for your daughter's hand, not her paw."

"Golo!" bellowed the King. "I command you to marry her. Come back here!" But Duke Golo had already darted through the door and was making his way in all haste down the corridor.

King Hugo stormed at the cat for having lost him such a desirable son-in-law. But next came Count Bohamel de Braise, and the King once again tried to put a fair face on bad fortune. Though his estates were not as large as Golo's, Bohamel was a harsh overlord and what he lacked in land he made up in taxing his tenants; and, at this match, King Hugo would have been well satisfied.

However, when Count Bohamel saw Margot, he threw back his head and gave a rasping laugh:

"Majesty, you make sport of me. Some wives have been called cats, but no cat's been called wife. Look at her claws! They'd tear the bedsheets to ribbons. If I ever dared embrace her, she'd scratch me to the bone."

"Your claws are sharper than mine," said Margot. "Ask your tenants."

No matter how King Hugo commanded or cajoled, pleaded or threatened, Bohamel would have no part of marriage with a cat-princess.

"Your misfortune is your own, and not mine," he told the King, and strode from the chamber.

The same happened with the suitors who followed. Each, in turn, found one pretext or another:

"Good heavens, Majesty," protested the Marquis de Cabasson, shuddering. "With a wife like that, I could never invite my friends to dine. She'd never use the proper fork. And what a breach of etiquette when she drank from a saucer."

"I daresay your friends would be too deep in their cups," answered Margot, "to notice what I did with a saucer."

"A cat-wife?" sneered the Seigneur de Malcourir. "She'd dance on the rooftops with every passing tom."

"I assure you," said Margot, "my virtue's greater than yours."

By this time, word had spread through the palace that King Hugo's daughter had become a cat. The councillors and ministers gossiped, the court ladies tittered, the footmen snickered, the kitchen maids giggled; and soon all in the palace were whispering behind their hands or laughing up their sleeves.

"See what you've done!" cried the King. "Shamed me! Humiliated me!"

"How so?" asked Margot. "I'm not ashamed of being a cat. Are you ashamed of being a king?"

King Hugo threw himself down on a chair and held his head in his hands. Not only had his daughter turned into a cat, it was now plain to him she would also turn into a spinster; and instead of a profitable marriage, there would be none at all. He began groaning miserably, blaming his daughter's stubbornness for putting him in such a plight.

That moment, the Court Chamberlain announced the suitors had departed, all but one: Count Raimond.

"How dare he come here?" exclaimed the King. "He's as pigheaded as my daughter—no, no, I don't mean that. Go fetch him, then." He turned to Margot. "Let the fellow see for himself what you've done. You've outwitted yourself this time, my girl. Marry you? One look and he'll change his tune. But at any rate, I'll have seen the last of him."

Alarmed at this, it was all Princess Elena could do to keep silent in her hiding place. She had never expected Raimond to present himself at court, knowing her father would only refuse him. Now she remembered Margot's warning. If Raimond, too, believed her a cat, indeed her heart would break. Margot, sensing her anguish, dangled her tail over the edge of the couch and waved the tip like a cautioning finger.

The Chamberlain ushered in Count Raimond. To Elena, he had never looked handsomer nor had she loved him so much; and she burned to go to him then and there. But worse than a broken heart was not knowing the strength of his love for her. So, tormented though she was, she bravely held her tongue.

At the sight of the cat, Raimond halted. He stood silent a long moment before he said to King Hugo:

"What I heard of Princess Elena I took for idle gossip. Now I see it is true."

With that, he stepped forward and bowed to Margot. Taking her paw in his hand, he said:

"Why, Princess, how well you look today. What a marvelous color your fur is. The stripes set it off to perfection. Your paws are softer than velvet. And what handsome whiskers, fine as threads of silk. You're beautiful as a cat as you were beautiful as a woman."

"What are you saying?" burst out King Hugo. "Have you gone mad? Paying court to a cat?"

"She's still my beloved as much as she's still your daughter," answered Raimond. "Do true lovers part because the hair of one goes white or the back of the other goes bent? Because the cheeks of one may wither, or the eyes of the other may dim? So long as her heart stays unchanged, so shall mine."

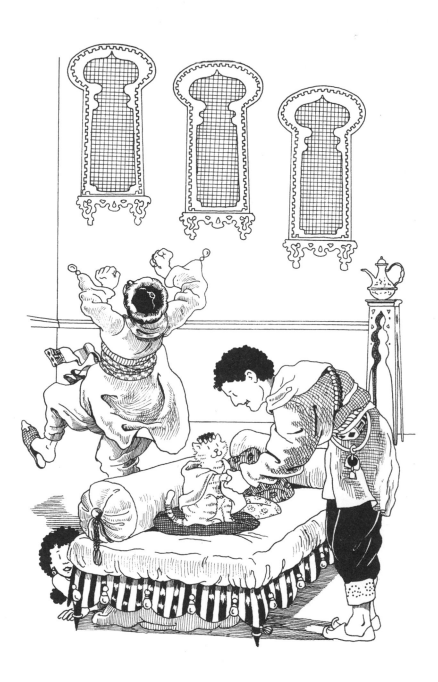

"Do you mean to tell me you'd marry her anyway?" cried King Hugo. "You, stand as bridegroom? And I, give her away? She'd make both of us look like fools."

"Majesty," said Raimond, "the only one who can make you look a fool is yourself. Yes, I will marry her if she will have it so. As for you, can it be that you love your daughter less than I love my intended? And yourself more than anyone else?"

At this, King Hugo began blustering and grumbling again. But, after a moment, he hung his head in shame. Finally, he said:

"My daughter is my daughter, whatever ill has befallen her; and I would have helped her least when she needed me the most. Well, Count of Albiclair, you're not the son-in-law I'd have chosen; but the choice was never mine in the first place. Marry, the two of you, if that's what you want. I still don't give a fig for your lute-plucking and verse-scribbling; but I do give you my blessing."

For her part, Elena was overjoyed at these words, and more than ever assured that Raimond was her true love. Again, she was about to leave her hiding place when, to her dismay, she heard Margot reply:

"Alas, there can be no wedding. Our marriage is out of the question."

"What do you mean?" roared King Hugo,

now as determined to see his daughter wed Raimond as he had been against it. "You bedeviled me to give my consent. Now you have it."

"By your own decree, cats are against the law," said Margot. "How shall Raimond keep me as a wife when it's forbidden to keep a cat?"

"Blast the decree!" retorted the King. "That's the stupidest thing I ever heard of. I made that law, so I can change it. From this day on, cats are welcome everywhere, even in my palace. In fact, I'll proclaim a new law that all my subjects must obey: everyone must keep a cat."

"No, Majesty," answered Margot. "Only let cats freely choose their people, and people choose their cats, and we shall get along very well."

At this, Princess Elena sprang out from under the couch and threw her arms around the bewildered but joyful Raimond.

And King Hugo commanded all the bells to be rung for the betrothal of the two lovers.

Instead of being angry at Margot for having tricked him, King Hugo kept his word, and better. He invited every cat in the kingdom to the wedding; and set out for them tables laden with bowls of cream, platters of fish and fowl, and bouquets of catnip. And Margot, as Maid of Honor, carried the bride's train.

King Hugo also repealed his other foolish laws. Though he grew no fonder of pickled herrings or holidays, he never again forbade them to his subjects. And because he saw to it that all cats were treated with utmost respect, he became known throughout the land as Hugo the Cat-King, a title which hardly pleased him but which he accepted nevertheless.

In gratitude, the Princess would have kept Margot in silks and jewels; but the cat politely declined, saying she was quite comfortable in her own fur. While she stayed with Elena and Raimond happily all their lives, having seen the ways of kings and courtiers, Margot privately judged it far more sensible to be a cat.

THE PRINCESS AND THE PEA

Hans Christian Andersen
Retold by Fiona Waters

The King and the Queen were not happy with the Prince. He was supposed to be finding himself a princess to marry, but he did seem to be incredibly fussy. He had traveled the land up and down and roundabout, but had returned home without a bride. Above all he wanted a REAL princess—a proper princess who was kind to children and animals, who could curtsy gracefully, and who wore a crown, even on Tuesdays. He had met plenty of princesses—but they were either too old or too young, too tall or too short, too silly or too serious. So he had come home and taken up gardening. The Queen gave up all hope that he would *ever* get married, especially now that his knees were always grubby and his hands dirty.

One night there was the most terrible storm. Thunder and lightning rolled and flashed around the palace, which was cold and drafty, and the candles kept blowing out. Everyone from the King to the under-parlormaid and the kitchen cat sat closer to the huge log fires burning in the Great Hall. In a lull between the claps of thunder, a gentle knock was heard at the front door. Everyone looked at each other in amazement. Who could possibly be out on such a dreadful night? The butler opened the door a fraction and squinted out.

There stood a princess, absolutely dripping wet from head to toe. At least she *said* she was a princess, but frankly no one believed her. Her velvet cloak looked like a soggy old blanket, her shoes squelched as she walked, and rain was dripping off the end of her nose. And yet she insisted that she was a princess, apologizing again and again for disturbing everyone on such a night.

As the visitor dried out by the fire the Prince could see she was very pretty, *and* her shoes had gold heels, *and* she knew just how to tickle the kitchen cat under his chin. The Prince gazed into her very blue eyes and grinned broadly.

The Queen frowned, but told the butler to make the girl a mug of cocoa, and she went off with the housekeeper and the smallest maid to make the bed in the second-best guest bedroom. (She wasn't going to use the best guest bedroom for someone who might, after all, only be a mere duchess.) First the smallest maid and the housekeeper took all the blankets and sheets off the bed, then they removed the mattress. The Queen placed a small pea, very carefully, in the center of the wooden base. Then the smallest maid and the housekeeper piled twenty mattresses on top of the pea. Twenty eiderdowns followed that, and finally a sheepskin blanket and a fine silk undersheet. It was so high that, when she went to bed later, the Princess (if indeed she was one) needed a long ladder to climb up to the top.

The next morning the Queen was up bright and early. After the smallest maid had brought her a cup of fragrant China tea, the Queen slipped into the Princess's room. To the Queen's surprise the Princess (if indeed she was one) was already awake. She was sitting in front of the mirror brushing her hair. She looked quite awful. She had great dark smudges under her eyes and was yawning most dreadfully.

"Well, my dear, how did you sleep?" asked the Queen sweetly.

"I am sorry to be so discourteous, but I have never had such a ghastly night in all my life. I didn't sleep a wink," said the Princess sadly. "It felt as though I were lying on a huge rock. I must be bruised from head to toe!"

Then the Queen knew she really *must* be a princess. Only a REAL princess could be so sensitive as to feel a tiny pea through all those layers.

The Queen was delighted. She rushed off to tell the King, who was even more delighted. And the Prince was positively overjoyed—especially when the Princess had recovered enough to tell him she was very interested in gardens, although she would never dream of getting her own hands dirty, of course. They were married as soon as possible and everyone lived happily—and comfortably—ever after.

Acknowledgments

The publisher would like to thank the copyright holders for permission to reproduce the following copyright material:

Joan Aiken: "The Spider in the Bath" from *The Last Slice of Rainbow and other stories* by Joan Aiken, Jonathan Cape 1985. Copyright © Joan Aiken Enterprises Ltd 1985. Reprinted by permission of Brandt & Brandt Literary Agents Inc. **Lloyd Alexander**: "The Cat-King's Daughter" from *The Town Cats and Other Tales* by Lloyd Alexander, E.P. Dutton 1977. Copyright © Lloyd Alexander 1977. Reprinted by permission of Dutton Children's Books, an imprint of Penguin Putnam Books for Young Readers, a division of Penguin Putnam Inc. **Margaret Baker**: "The Princess's Handkerchiefs" from *Tell Them Again Tales* by Margaret Baker, Hodder and Stoughton Ltd 1980. Copyright © Margaret Baker 1933. Reprinted by permission of Hodder and Stoughton Ltd. **Judy Corbalis**: "The Wrestling Princess" from *The Wrestling Princess and other stories* by Judy Corbalis, André Deutsch Ltd. 1986. Copyright © Judy Corbalis 1986. Reprinted by permission of the author. **Wendy Eyton**: "The Princess Who Met the North Wind" from *Tales from the Threepenny Bit* by Wendy Eyton, William Collins Sons & Co. Ltd. 1990. Copyright © Wendy Eyton 1990. Reprinted by permission of the author. **Eleanor Farjeon**: "The Seventh Princess" from *The Little Bookroom* by Eleanor Farjeon, Oxford University Press 1955. Copyright © Eleanor Farjeon 1955. Reprinted by permission of David Higham Associates Ltd. **Vivian French**: "The Princess and the Frog" by Vivian French. Copyright © Vivian French 2001. Reprinted by permission of the author. **Virginia Haviland**: "The Sleeping Beauty in the Wood" from *Favorite Fairy Tales Told Around the World* by Virginia Haviland. Copyright © 1985 by Virginia Haviland; copyright © 1985 by S. D. Schindler. Reprinted by permission of Little, Brown and Company (Inc.). **Geraldine McCaughrean**: "Mousey and Sulky Puss" from *Princess Stories*, Doubleday, a division of Transworld Publishers 1997. Copyright © Geraldine McCaughrean 1997. Reprinted by permission of Transworld Publishers Ltd. All rights reserved. **Pamela Oldfield**: "The Terribly Plain Princess" from *The Terribly Plain Princess and Other Stories*, Hodder and Stoughton Ltd. 1977. Copyright © Pamela Oldfield 1977. Reprinted by permission of the author c/o Watson, Little Ltd. **Fiona Waters**: "The Twelve Dancing Princesses" and "The Princess and the Pea." Copyright © Fiona Waters 2001. Reprinted by permission of the author. **Jay Williams**: "Petronella" from *The Practical Princess and other Liberating Fairy Tales* by Jay Williams. Published by Parents Magazine Press. Copyright © 1978 by Jay Williams. Reprinted by permission of Scholastic Inc.

Every effort has been made to obtain permission to reproduce copyright material but there may be cases where we have been unable to trace a copyright holder. The publisher will be happy to correct any omissions in future printings.

Titles in the
Kingfisher Treasury series

~